*You haven't seen the last of me . . .*

"I'm going home now. But you haven't seen the last of me," Darlene told Hailey. "Robert Q Parker the third needs to learn that Darlene Riggs isn't a *toy*." Her lips formed a thin, straight line. "He can't just toss me away. He made promises." The thin, straight line became a smile without humor. "It isn't nice to break promises."

The smile chilled Hailey to the bone.

Terrifying thrillers by Diane Hoh:

*Funhouse*

*The Accident*

*The Invitation*

*The Train*

*The Fever*

*Nightmare Hall: The Silent Scream*

*Nightmare Hall: The Roommate*

*Nightmare Hall: Deadly Attraction*

and coming soon . . .

*Nightmare Hall: The Wish*

# NIGHTMARE HALL

## Deadly Attraction

## DIANE HOH

SCHOLASTIC INC.
New York Toronto London Auckland Sydney

No part of this publication may be reproduced in whole or in
part, or stored in a retrieval system, or transmitted in any form
or by any means, electronic, mechanical, photocopying, record-
ing, or otherwise, without written permission of the publisher.
For information regarding permission, write to Scholastic Inc.,
730 Broadway, New York, NY 10003.

ISBN 0-590-46015-3

12 11 10 9 8 7 6 5 4 3 2 1          3 4 5 6 7 8/9

Printed in the U.S.A.                    01

First Scholastic printing, September 1993

# NIGHTMARE HALL

## HALL

*Deadly Attraction*

# Prologue

Each time Hailey watched the scene play in slow-motion in her mind, her stomach would churn and her pulse would race and her heart would begin thudding violently in her chest.

Because she knew what was coming.

She would close her eyes and try to stop it, try to make it end, but it wouldn't.

It would play on . . .

She was at Burgers Etc. It was the night Darlene Riggs and Robert Q Parker, III, first met. Tray in hand, Darlene glided slowly around the room in her black shorts and white T-shirt, slowly, so slowly. Robert Q's head turned, bit by bit, following her every move and the line of her body.

It should have been a night like any other.

But it wasn't. Because it had been the beginning . . .

The beginning of all the horror.

# Prologue

# Chapter 1

Hailey Kingman, a freshman at Salem University, was at Burgers Etc., a popular campus hangout, on the chilly night in early November when Robert Q Parker met Darlene Riggs.

Robert Q, blond and smooth, in his letterman's jacket, was a sophomore and a B.M.O.C. — a Big Man on Campus — at Salem. Darlene wasn't a student at Salem, but she'd grown up in Twin Falls. She was cute, with short, dark, curly hair and a round but too heavily made-up face. Her uniform of black shorts and white T-shirt fit her curves nicely, bringing a glow of appreciation to Robert's eyes. Those eyes followed Darlene's every move with relish as she dashed, tray and order pad in hand, from booth to booth in the noisy, crowded diner. Robert Q's friends seemed amused by his interest in the waitress.

Hailey and *her* friends found their attention

drawn to Robert Q's table. "*Look* at him!" Hailey's roommate, Nell Riley, declared in disgust. "He's practically drooling!"

"He *is* drooling," Hailey said, reaching up to smooth her wavy, shoulder-length, strawberry-blonde hair. "But then, so is *she*. She knows he's watching her, and she loves it."

Nell nodded. "I heard he broke up with Gerrie Northrup. Or vice versa. I see her over there in the corner, looking very cozy with Richard Wentworth."

"I thought Richard was Robert Q's best friend," Hailey said.

The dark-haired girl sitting beside her shrugged. "Share and share alike," Jessica Vogt said. "Or maybe Robert Q is slavering over that waitress in hopes of making Gerrie jealous."

Ian Banion, Jess's boyfriend, laughed. "Am I imagining things, or is no one at this table a member of the Robert Q Parker fan club?"

"*You're* not, are you?" Hailey asked. She had only recently met Jess and Ian, residents of an off-campus dorm, Nightingale Hall, and didn't know them that well.

Ian's long, dark hair swept his shoulders as he shook his head. "No way. The guy's a jerk. Always tossing money around as if he owned his own bank. He talks too loud, drives like a maniac, and gives new meaning to the term pushy."

Hailey nodded. "Yeah, but I guess it works for him. He's a star on the tennis team, he manages the campus radio station, he belongs to the best fraternity on campus, and look at the crew of fans surrounding him." Robert's booth was crowded with "beautiful people."

"I still say he's a pain in the butt," Ian said firmly.

They all watched as the waitress, whose name tag read *DARLENE RIGGS*, approached Robert Q's table. They heard her say eagerly, "May I take your order?" and heard Robert Q's laugh and his, "Honey, you can take anything you want. Help yourself."

Hailey and Nell rolled their eyes heavenward.

The girl answered with a coquettish smile. She looked pleased.

"She's *flattered*," Nell said, revulsion dripping from her words. "Can you believe it?"

"She definitely looks interested," Jess said calmly. "But then, why not? He's a Big Man on Campus. And you know how smooth he can be when he lays on the charm."

"B.M.O.C. or not," Hailey grumbled, watching Darlene taking food and drink orders while Robert Q openly leered at her, "he's got the perception and sensitivity of a Q-Tip. He's turning that poor girl on just to rattle Gerrie's cage. It's repulsive."

But the waitress didn't seem to mind. Her smile as she served the table was radiant. Her short hair bobbed energetically around her fair-skinned face as she hurried back and forth from table to kitchen and back again, carrying loaded trays.

"I have to admit, she sure does fill out that uniform in all the right places," Nell said. There was more than a trace of envy in her voice. Nell was pretty: dark-haired, with fine, even features in an oval face and beautiful, thickly-lashed dark eyes. An accomplished gymnast, she was rail-thin and, as she herself regretfully put it, "When I stand sideways, I look like a *door*."

"I can't believe the way Robert Q is ogling her," Hailey said, irritably tapping the laminated table top with her metal spoon. "Like he's ready for dessert and she's a double-fudge brownie."

"He's going to ask her to meet him after her shift," Jess said matter-of-factly. "And she's going to say she'd love to. Just look at her face! She's in heaven."

"Well," Hailey responded, "if that waitress is looking for a knight on a white charger, someone should warn her that Robert Q's shining armor is slightly tarnished."

"*More* than slightly," Jess agreed.

"Before he and Gerrie got together," Hailey said, "he dated and discarded girls like used tissues. His little black book must be the size of an unabridged dictionary."

"Yeah, with his name in place of the definition for *jerk*," Nell said. After a moment or two of silence, her eyes on Darlene, she added, "One of these days, maybe *he'll* get dumped. I'd love to see that. Think that waitress is the right candidate?"

"Definitely not," Jess said. "She looks like she just won the lottery."

They sat in silence, sipping their drinks. Hailey couldn't take her eyes off the mini-drama centering around Robert Q's table. The waitress . . . Darlene? . . . seemed so happy, so delighted by Robert Q's outrageous flirting. Couldn't she *tell* what he *was*?

I'm not being fair, she scolded. Robert Q is good-looking, well-dressed, and he must have *some* charm or he'd be sitting in his dorm room alone nights instead of tooling around all over Twin Falls in his little Miata with a gorgeous female at his side.

Maybe I'm jealous, she thought, sighing. I've only had four dates since I hit Salem University's campus, and none of them made my toes tingle.

Hailey loved college. Salem University's campus was beautiful, green and rolling and wooded, the old but solid buildings stone or brick, some festooned with lush green ivy. Her roommate, Nell, was the best, and most of her classes were interesting. After years of being raised by a strict grandmother following the death of her parents in a car wreck when she was eight years old, she was especially happy to be living on her own.

But it would be nice to have someone . . . special . . . to share all of this with. Those years in her grandmother's big, empty house had been lonely ones.

What is it with me, anyway? she wondered. Does my appearance shout B-O-R-I-N-G? Why is it that guys I go out with want to know what I think about the Middle East or if I consider global warming a serious threat? Couldn't I, just once, go out with someone who tells me jokes and laughs at my jokes? Someone like . . . like that guy over there, leaning against the wall talking with Pete Torrance. "That guy over there" was tall, thin, with dark hair and a strong, angled face. His eyes, Hailey decided, were probably brown, maybe with a touch of green. Pete, a sophomore who lived in Hailey's dorm, was shorter, with powerful shoulders and chest, and blond hair cut very short. They were both watching the unfolding scenario involving Robert Q and the waitress. Both looked thoroughly disgusted.

Good. That meant that neither of them was an insensitive pig.

Ian, noticing where Hailey's eyes were, said, "That's Finn Conran with Pete Torrance. He's a lowly freshman, too. Works here. Clean-up, fix-it, that kind of stuff. The guy is pretty sharp. Pete might hang out with Robert Q's crowd sometimes, but I'll bet Finn doesn't. That crowd wouldn't be his type." Ian grinned slyly and said, "I don't think he's dating anyone."

Hailey flushed, wishing Ian hadn't noticed who she'd been watching. "I don't even know the guy," she said defensively.

But she thought she might *like* to.

As they all turned their attention back to Robert Q's booth, it was clear to everyone at Hailey's table that Darlene was mouthing the words, "See you later" in Robert Q's direction.

"Oh, no," Nell groaned, "she *fell* for it! That's another notch on Robert Q's belt."

Ian shrugged. "Short of lassoing her and holding her prisoner in the Dungeon at the Quad, I don't think anyone could have stopped her. Robert Q may be a jerk, but he's a smooth jerk. She's not the first girl to fall for his act, and she won't be the last."

"No," Hailey said reluctantly, "but from the look on that girl's face, I'll bet she hopes she'll be the last."

So, when Darlene came to their booth, Hailey was especially nice to her, asking her name, introducing her to everyone at their table. What she *really* wanted to do was warn the girl away from Robert Q. But she knew that was hopeless. It was too late.

As they were leaving, Hailey glanced toward the spot where Pete and the dark-haired boy — Finn — had been. They were both gone. She was very annoyed with them for disappearing.

And even more annoyed with herself for caring.

I don't even *know* Finn. He could be more of a creep than Robert Q.

No. Not possible.

That poor girl . . . Darlene. Did she have any idea what she was getting into?

# Chapter 2

Two nights later, Hailey had just finished blow-drying her hair in the second floor bathroom at Devereaux Hall, when Darlene came into the room. She was wearing tight jeans and a form-fitting, too-bright yellow sweater. An excess of blusher and several thick coats of mascara gave Darlene's round, pretty face an unnatural mannequin look.

She doesn't *need* so much makeup, Hailey thought.

"Hi!" the girl said brightly, setting a thick red clutch bag on the shelf beneath the mirror. "I'm Darlene Riggs. And you're the girl who was so nice to me the other night at the diner. Halley?"

"Hailey."

"Hailey. Right. I'm here with Robert Q Parker," she said, beaming. "He doesn't *live* here. He lives at the Sigma Chi house. We're just visiting one of his friends." Darlene smiled dreamily. "Isn't Robert Q something? I can't believe he asked me out."

"Yeah, he's something, all right." Hailey had to bite her tongue to keep from adding exactly what she thought that something was.

Darlene began to add yet another coat of mascara to her lashes. "I know the girl Robert Q was dating before me. Well, I don't *know* her, but I've seen them together. They came into the diner a lot." She sighed. "She's very sophisticated."

"Right," Hailey snapped, annoyed with Darlene for admiring Gerrie, who had the depth of a pancake.

"I wish I could do my hair like yours, in that French braid kind of thing." Darlene aimed a face of disgust at her mirror reflection. "I don't suppose you'd have time to give me some tips? On how to look more chic?"

Hailey often wore her strawberry-blonde hair in a French braid because of its natural curl. If it wasn't restrained, it frizzed around her face like coiled wire.

"I wouldn't ask," Darlene added shyly as she teased her hair into a thick froth, "but you were so friendly the other night."

Meaning, Hailey thought, that I didn't snub her. Which probably meant that Robert Q's crowd wasn't exactly embracing Darlene. No surprise there. Susan Grossbeck, Lindsey Kite, and Puffy Wycroft weren't known for their generosity of spirit. As for Lyle Sutton and Richard Wentworth, Robert Q's best buddies, they'd think this whole thing with Darlene was hilarious.

While she was trying to figure out how to warn Darlene away from Robert Q, Darlene rambled on. "My old boyfriend, Bo Jessup, wasn't anything like Robert Q. We went together all through school. Bo was quarterback on the football team, and I was a cheerleader. Bo was so good, he almost got a scholarship to Salem. But," her voice flattened, "he didn't. Now he works in his father's garage. He was pretty upset when I broke up with him a couple of weeks ago."

Hailey tossed her damp towel into the laundry hamper. "Then he must be pretty ticked at you for going out with Robert Q."

Darlene nodded. "That's for sure. He thinks I *belong* to him, like I'm his personal property. That jealousy of his always made me crazy. If I so much as *talked* to another boy, Bo would go after him." She shrugged. "So yeah, he's pretty mad right now. But I told him, I have to think of my future. Bo's never going to get out of that garage. We both know that. And washing oil-stained coveralls for the rest of my life is not what I want." Darlene turned toward Hailey. "So, what do you say? Could you give me some pointers on how to look more so-phisticated?"

"I'm not so sure I know very much about sophistication," Hailey said. "But I'd be glad to help. I'm in room 242. Just knock on the door if you want to talk. You'll have to pound. My roommate believes a stereo is worthless if it's not at full blast. Stop in any time."

In the hallway, Hailey immediately regret-ted her offer. She didn't even *know* Dar-lene. Besides, look who the girl was *dating*. Robert Q!

But were they really dating, as Darlene clearly thought they were? Or was Robert Q just *using* Darlene to make Gerrie Northrup jealous?

And what about Darlene's ex-boyfriend? She'd said he was the jealous type, who "went after" boys Darlene had only talked to. What would he do to someone she was actually *dating*?

Hailey shuddered. The newspapers and tele-vision were full of stories about ex-boyfriends doing terrible things to estranged girlfriends.

"That girl is going to get hurt," Hailey an-nounced as she entered a cramped but sunny room 242, where Nell was stretched out on her bed, quietly studying. The stereo was, surprisingly, silent.

Nell lifted her head, and regarded Hailey with dark eyes behind wire-rimmed glasses. "*What* girl?"

"Darlene Riggs. Remember? The waitress at Burgers, the one Robert Q was making a play for the other night." Hailey filled Nell in on the bathroom encounter.

When she'd finished, Nell shook her head sadly. "Can you imagine the number Puffy and Susan and Lindsey are going to do on that girl? Making fun of her clothes and hair and her makeup? They'll reduce her to cracker crumbs."

"That's why I said I'd help her." Anticipating Nell's reaction, Hailey studied her fingernails.

Nell's jaw dropped. "You did *what*?"

Hailey retreated to her bed and sat, cross-legged, on the colorful quilt. "She asked me if I'd give her some pointers, help her look more sophisticated . . . as if *I* know! But I said I'd try. She seems very nice, Nell."

"You're going to help the girl who's dating that slime, Robert Q?"

"Well, that's just it," Hailey said, spreading her hands helplessly in front of her, "Is he really *dating* her? I mean, does he even *like* this girl, or is he just using her? She also said her ex-boyfriend is pretty crazed over their breakup. So she could use someone on her side. Why not us?"

Bolting upright, Nell jabbed an angry finger in the air. "How do you *do* that? How do you go from *your* offer of help to the word 'us' without blinking an eye? I, Ellen Marie Riley, was not *present* in that bathroom when you so generously offered your services, remember? *I* offered *nothing*. . . . zilch, *nada*!"

With that, Nell returned to her textbook.

Some thirty minutes later, Hailey opened the door to a knock and found Darlene standing in the hall. "Okay if we talk now?" she asked, and Hailey nodded.

"I know who *you* are," Darlene told Nell, who was feigning a lack of interest in the new arrival. "You're the gymnast. I've seen you perform. You're really good."

Hailey grinned. If that didn't win Nell over, nothing would. And Darlene wasn't just jerking Nell's strings — she was totally sincere.

"So," Nell said, sitting up, "what can we do?"

The three of them spent nearly an hour crowded together on Hailey's bed. Darlene talked nonstop about Robert Q, in a rushed, breathless voice, as if she'd known him forever, while Nell and Hailey, armed with brush, comb, hot rollers, and curling iron, experimented with Darlene's hair. Using every can and bottle of mousse and gel they possessed between them, the roommates managed to tame the brown curls into a smooth, more natural style.

Then they got to work on Darlene's makeup. First, she washed her face. Then Hailey bunched Darlene's hair into two silly little pigtails to pull it out of the way so she could work with blusher and mascara and the tiniest bit of eye shadow. The new makeup was applied with a very light touch.

The result was a fresh, very appealing, natural look.

"But," Nell joked, "those pigtails have got to go!"

They were still laughing when Robert Q suddenly opened the door and stood there, an annoyed look on his face. When he saw Darlene's hair arranged in pigtails sticking up behind each ear, his frown deepened. "What is *that*?" he cried.

"Some *people* are incredibly rude," Nell said in a haughty voice. "Didn't anyone ever teach you to knock?" As she spoke, she smiled sweetly at Darlene, who was struggling to remove the rubber bands from her hair.

"The door wasn't locked," Robert Q said,

striding over to yank at Darlene's head. She winced in pain as a rubber band, and with it several strands of dark brown hair, came off in his hand.

"Do something with your hair and let's get going," he barked. "Everyone's waiting."

It made Hailey sick, then, the way Darlene flushed and jumped up, her hands fumbling with her hair, and followed Robert Q out of the room, murmuring her thanks and her good-bye as she went. In the doorway, she half-turned to say quietly, "I wish you two were going to this party." Then Robert Q yanked on her hand and she was gone.

"Doesn't that just turn your stomach?" Nell cried as the door closed. "The way she trotted after him! Like a puppy."

"She really seems to think they're going to be together forever," Hailey said worriedly. "The way she went on and *on* about him . . ."

Nell shrugged. "She sure seems determined. Head over heels, that girl. Changing her hair, her makeup. I wouldn't do that for *any* guy, least of all someone like Robert Q."

Nell returned to her studying then. But the happy, expectant look on Darlene Riggs's face haunted Hailey's thoughts. She tried to concentrate on a math assignment, then an English paper due in a few days, but it was hopeless.

Darlene Riggs was going to get hurt.

And although she couldn't have said why, Hailey couldn't shake the weird feeling that something far worse than a simple broken heart was in the works.

# Chapter 3

Although Hailey found herself glancing around in classrooms and on campus, she only saw Pete Torrance's dark-haired friend once, near the student center with Pete. But she saw Darlene frequently, on campus with Robert Q and at the mall with Puffy, Susan, and Lindsey. Darlene always stopped for a few minutes to talk to Hailey. She seemed happy.

Hailey was surprised that Darlene's relationship with Robert Q was lasting so long. It had been two whole *weeks* and still he showed no sign of dumping her.

Then she didn't see Darlene for a while, and wondered if that meant that Robert Q had tired of her. Was Darlene home crying her eyes out? Hailey hoped not, for Darlene's sake, although she couldn't help feeling that *any* girl would be better off without Robert Q.

Hailey and Nell were invited by Pete Torrance to a party at the Sigma Chi house. Pete didn't belong, but he had friends who did.

Nell couldn't go because she had a gymnastics meet, but Hailey went with Jess and Ian. She was sitting in a corner with them when Robert Q arrived with a girl on his arm, a girl far more his usual type than Darlene.

Hailey stared in dismay.

The girl was sleek and slim, with smooth, shiny dark hair brushed up and away from her face. She was beautifully dressed in expensive rust-colored suede jeans and a silky cream-colored blouse. As the pair entered the room, she glanced up at Robert Q adoringly.

"Oh, no," Hailey breathed. "I *knew* it! He's dumped Darlene! She must be devastated!"

"That *is* Darlene, Hailey," Jess said.

Hailey stared. The girl with Robert Q grinned and waved.

"Haven't you seen her lately?" Jess asked.

"No, I . . . she looks so . . . different," Hailey said in a stunned voice. "I really didn't recognize her."

"A whole new woman," Ian said. Jess heard admiration in his voice and stabbed him with an elbow.

"I liked the *old* Darlene," Hailey grumbled.

"What this campus *doesn't* need is another Puffy or Susan or Lindsey. Darlene was an original. I liked that."

An hour later, Hailey was in the kitchen getting ice cubes, when a voice drifted in from out in the hall. "Did you *hear* what she said?" Puffy Wycroft's voice. No one else on campus whined like that. "She actually thinks Robert Q is going to give her his fraternity pin. Can you *believe* it? I nearly *died*! It was hard to keep a straight face."

"You *didn't* keep a straight face," Susan Grossbeck said. "You were smirking."

"Whatever."

Hailey's hand had frozen in midair between the refrigerator and her glass. They had to be talking about Darlene.

"Well, she doesn't know about Gerrie yet," Susan's voice came again. "I heard Robert Q tell Richard that what the townie didn't know wouldn't hurt her." She laughed. "So he's been taking her home and then meeting Gerrie afterwards, trying to work things out with her. Now that they've made peace, Darlene's out on her ear. Only *she* thinks she's about to be pinned. Can you believe how naive she is?"

Hailey was horrified. So Robert Q had only been playing with Darlene, just as Hailey'd suspected. His friends thought that was funny? Could people really be so cruel?

"Serves the girl right," Puffy said out in the hall. "Does she really think a new hairdo and suede jeans are all she needs? She's *still* just a diner waitress. Anyway," she added with a disdainful sniff, "when will these townies learn they don't belong with college boys? They should stick to their own kind."

Cold fury flooded Hailey as the voices moved away and faded. She leaned against the refrigerator door for support.

Someone came into the room.

A deep voice said, "Hey, you okay?"

Hailey looked up. It was that dark-haired guy, the one she'd seen at the diner with Pete Torrance. That night, she'd thought she wanted to meet him. But not now, not tonight. Darlene needed her.

"You okay?" he repeated. "Your face is the same color as that appliance you're hugging." When Hailey said nothing, he added, "I'm Finn Conran. Can I help? Are you sick?"

"No," Hailey finally managed.

But she *was* sick. Sick from thinking about Darlene expecting to be given the fraternity pin of a boy whose friends called her "the townie." What would Darlene do when instead, Robert Q dumped her?

Hailey lifted her head and looked into Finn

Conran's eyes. They were, as she'd imagined, brown. A warm, chestnut brown. With green flecks. "You aren't by any chance a friend of Robert Q's, are you?"

"You've *got* to be kidding," was his answer.

"Good! Well, then, I'm Hailey Kingman. And I'm sorry, but right now I have to go find someone. Excuse me."

What was important was finding Darlene.

She had no idea what she would say when she found her. No matter how carefully she phrased the truth, her words would slice Darlene into a thousand pieces.

Hailey reluctantly returned to the raucous, crowded, massive living room in the big, old house, and immediately realized with a sickening lurch of her stomach that she might not have to search for the right words, after all.

Because Darlene was sitting alone, her back rigid, on a wooden chair off to one side of the area cleared for dancing. Her eyes, wide with disbelief, were fixed on Robert Q.

He was on the dance floor, his arms tightly wrapped around Gerrie Northrup, elegant in a blue silk halter dress. Her head was nestled cozily against Robert Q's shoulder. His head rested on hers. The two seemed totally unaware of Darlene's eyes on them.

They look like someone *glued* them together, Hailey thought with renewed rage. And Darlene looks like she's being stabbed repeatedly with a very sharp knife.

Hailey hurried over to crouch beside Darlene's chair.

Never taking her eyes off the entwined couple, Darlene said in an emotionless monotone, "That's a really pretty sweater, Hailey. Blue is your color. You should wear it all the time." She turned toward Hailey then. Her eyes were bright with unshed tears.

"Darlene," Hailey said, placing a gentle hand on Darlene's arm, "it's okay."

A sudden commotion at the front door caught their attention. Hailey looked up to see a guy the size of a small mountain shouldering his way through the crowd. He was headed straight for Darlene, his square face dark with anger. His thick, dark brows were drawn together in a scowl, his jaw jutting forth with grim determination.

"Bo!" Darlene jumped to her feet. "What are you *doing* here?"

Hailey, too, stood up. So . . . the ex-boyfriend. Had Robert Q even noticed the new arrival? Hailey glanced toward the couple, still entwined on the dance floor. *Her* guess would be that Bo Jessup could probably drag Darlene by her hair from the frat house without Robert Q lifting a finger to stop him. But Robert Q *was* watching now. He looked mildly interested.

Hailey had never seen anyone as red-hot with anger as Darlene's ex-boyfriend. And he was certainly big enough to reduce to kitty litter anyone dumb enough to get in his way. What was it Darlene had said? Something about Bo going after any boy she talked to. . . . And Darlene and Robert had done a lot more than just talk.

Bo parked himself directly in front of a red-faced, open-mouthed Darlene. "There!" he shouted, drawing the attention of all the party guests as he pointed at Robert Q, "are you satisfied now? You see what a worm the guy is? Hitting on another girl right in front of you. He's a pig, Dar. Where's your pride? Are you too stupid to know when you're not wanted? I want you to come with me. *Now!*"

Tears flooded Darlene's eyes. Her cheeks were blazing. "Bo, please . . ." Then her voice hardened. "I'm *not* leaving."

"You don't *belong* here." He hadn't lowered his voice. Snickering and giggling sounded throughout the room. "Come with me now, Dar. My truck's right outside."

From somewhere behind Hailey, Puffy Wycroft said loudly, "Now how did I *know* this guy had a truck?"

And Richard Wentworth, looking amused, said, "The townie looks pretty shook. But if you ask me, this guy is perfect for her. He can sling her over his shoulder and haul her away caveman-style. Townies probably like that kind of stuff."

He was silenced by an icy look from Hailey.

Bo didn't sling Darlene over his shoulder. Instead, after giving her one last look, which Hailey interpreted as half-plea, half-contempt, he turned on his heel and made his way back through the crowd. When he reached the front door, he whirled to shout, "I'll be waiting outside by the truck. You *show* up, Darlene. These people will just chew you up and spit you out."

Suddenly, he whirled and stomped over to Robert Q, still standing with Gerrie on the dance floor, an amused smile on his face. The smile quickly faded as Bo approached.

"You stay away from Darlene, you hear me?" Bo shouted, waving a fist in Robert Q's face. "She's too good for the likes of you. If I catch you near her, I'll turn you into Silly Putty, and that's a promise!"

Someone tittered as he spun away from Robert Q, and Bo's head jerked up in response. His dark eyes swept the room. "Go ahead, laugh!" he said coldly. "But I'll be the one having the last laugh!"

# Chapter 4

There was complete silence then as Bo strode out of the room.

The door had barely closed after him when Darlene spun away from Hailey and rushed out of the room.

There was a heavy sigh of relief from the crowd. Scattered applause followed Darlene's exit. Hailey's eyes blazed in a sweeping, disgusted glare that silenced every snickering, applauding onlooker it grazed. Then, through an indignant silence, she ran after Darlene.

Behind her, Robert Q and Gerrie resumed dancing.

Hailey found Darlene in the downstairs bathroom. She was standing in front of the mirror, staring into it. She had stopped crying. As Hailey entered, Darlene's hands reached up to touch her new hairdo, then slid down to pat her perfectly applied makeup.

"Darlene . . ." Hailey began.

But she stopped when Darlene turned to her with bewildered eyes to ask, "What did I do wrong?"

"You didn't do *anything*," Hailey said vehemently. "It's him, Darlene. He's a total slime."

Darlene shook her head. "No, no, he *isn't*. Robert Q is smart and sophisticated. And he's so popular. How could he be so popular if he was slime, Hailey? *Everyone* knows Robert Q."

"That doesn't mean they *like* him," Hailey said sharply. "He's a jerk."

But Darlene wasn't listening. "It's that *girl*," she said angrily, her eyes narrowing. "She went after Robert Q tonight, when she knew he was with me." She looked at Hailey. "Does she expect me to just wimp out and let her *have* him?"

"Darlene! What you should do is go back out there and have a good time. Don't let them see how upset you are. There are lots of guys out there who would *kill* to dance with you. Please, Darlene. Go have fun. And tell Robert Q to take a hike."

"She's not going to get away with this," Darlene vowed, as if Hailey hadn't spoken. "He loves *me*. He *said* so. I'll go back out there, all right. I'll rescue Robert Q from that tarantula.

Believe me, Hailey, he'll be grateful."

Hailey gave up. Darlene wasn't going to listen to anything she had to say.

They were about to leave the bathroom when, for the second time that night, Hailey heard unwelcome voices from a distance.

Darlene heard the voices, too. Her face lit up. "That's Robert Q!" she cried. "He's come looking for me. See, Hailey, I *told* you!"

But then they heard Robert Q's voice as clearly as if it were being broadcast over a PA system. "Look, Richard, twenty bucks is my final offer. You take the townie home. Get her out of here. Just drop her at her house. It's on Fourth Street. Not that far. Twenty bucks for twenty minutes, that's not bad."

Hailey froze. Her eyes went to Darlene, who was listening carefully.

"Why can't she go home with that hunk of lunk with the truck?" Richard Wentworth's voice whined. "He *wants* to take her home. You wouldn't even have to pay him. Anyway, why should I leave you a clear field with Gerrie? I was making real progress with her until you decided to dump the townie."

"Twenty-five," Robert Q said, "and that's my top offer. It's highway robbery, but Gerrie says either Darlene goes or *she* goes." He laughed. "No contest. And face it, Wentworth," he added, "you're not in Gerrie's league."

Richard gave in. "Okay, okay! I'll get the townie off your hands. C'mon, time flies. Let's go get her before I change my mind."

The voices ended.

In the silence that followed, Hailey searched frantically for comforting words, but found none.

Darlene's face was stark-white. But her eyes blazed. "Did I hear that right?" she asked Hailey, her voice low. "He thinks he can just hand me over to someone else? He goes running back to Gerrie and gives *me* to that cretin, Richard? That *is* what I heard, isn't it?"

"Darlene — "

"No! Don't say a *word*, Hailey!" Darlene stood up very straight. "Not one word. I know what I heard." She picked up her purse. "If I were still in fifth grade, I'd get my big brother Mike after Robert Q and Richard. But I'm not in fifth grade anymore." Now her cheeks flamed with color. "I'm going home with Bo now. But you haven't seen the last of me, and that's a promise. Robert Q Parker the third needs to learn that Darlene Riggs isn't a *toy*." Her lips formed a thin, straight line. "He can't just toss me away. He made promises." The thin, straight line became a smile without humor. "It isn't nice to break promises."

The smile chilled Hailey to the bone.

"If Robert Q should ask," Darlene said coolly, "tell him I went home and that I'll explain when he calls me tomorrow. And," she added grimly, "if he knows what's good for him, he *will* call me tomorrow." Then, in a lighter voice, she added, "See you, Hailey. Have fun." And she hurried out of the room, leaving Hailey standing at the sink, with wide eyes and an open mouth.

Things had turned around so quickly, Hailey couldn't think straight. Darlene was going home with Bo? Was that smart? He'd been so angry . . . all those threats . . . was Darlene safe with him?

Telling herself that Darlene wasn't the one Bo had threatened, Hailey turned and followed Darlene from the room.

She had just left the restroom when Richard Wentworth, a petulant expression on his face, approached her in the hall.

"Hey, Hailey, you know that townie, right? I saw you talking to her earlier. You seen her anywhere?"

Hailey wanted to slap him. She wanted to slap *someone*. "If you mean Darlene Riggs," she said icily, "she was bored to death with this party. So she left."

Her irony was lost on Richard. He looked delighted. "Yeah? No kidding?"

Cretin! "No kidding. You just lost twenty-five bucks, Richard."

His mouth opened. "How did you . . . ?" Then he shrugged, grinned, and hurried back to the party.

When Hailey had rejoined Ian and Jess and filled them in on the disgusting details, she added, "Did you know that Darlene has a brother on campus? Do you know anyone named Mike Riggs?" Maybe, if she could explain Darlene's situation to her brother, he could talk some sense into his sister.

But they both shook their heads. "Didn't even know she *had* a brother," Ian said.

Hailey confessed, "I have this really bad feeling. I know it sounds stupid, but — "

"Oh, *please* don't say things like that!" Jess cried. "We're just getting over what happened to us at Nightingale Hall. Please, no dire premonitions of more trouble, Hailey."

Hailey knew all about the old, off-campus dorm. It had been nicknamed "Nightmare Hall" because a girl had been murdered there last spring. The death had been made to look like suicide, and all sorts of strange things had happened there. Jess's face still paled whenever the subject came up.

"Sorry, Jess," Hailey murmured. She couldn't shake the bad feeling, but that didn't mean she had to depress other people.

She began searching the noisy crowd for the dark-haired guy — Finn Conran. I should have talked to him when I had the chance, in the kitchen, she told herself. He probably thinks I'm a snob, like half the people at this party.

She spotted Pete Torrance talking to a girl in red. But there was no sign of Finn.

Maybe that's why I can't shake this feeling of doom, Hailey thought as she moved toward a tray of chips and dip and drinks. Maybe it's disappointment that I've blown an opportunity to get to know someone interesting.

But, a moment later, she realized that her premonition had nothing to do with Finn Conran.

Because a shout sounded from outside, then another and another, becoming louder and more urgent. The shouts were coming from behind Hailey's shoulder, where a large wooden porch ran the width of the house.

People turned to listen, to stare, and then, as the shouts continued, they began to move, murmuring and shoving, in one massed throng toward the door.

As the crowd reached her, Hailey became a part of it. Someone pushed the back door open and they swept out onto the porch.

Robert Q, still shouting for help, was kneeling on the lantern-lit back lawn, looking down at something. Something lying very still, an unmoving pile of blue silk . . .

"It's Gerrie," a girl behind Hailey said. "That's Gerrie Northrup on the ground."

Robert Q stopped calling for help and lifted his head as the crowd moved en masse down the wide wooden steps and out over the lawn. "I think she's dead," he said in an odd, strangled voice. "I think Gerrie's dead."

# Chapter 5

When it became clear that Gerrie Northrup was indeed unconscious, Pete Torrance ran back inside the Sigma Chi house to call for help.

"What happened to her?" Puffy cried, addressing Robert Q. "Is that *blood*? What did you *do* to her?"

Hailey could see a spreading pool of red under Gerrie's head.

"Don't be stupid, Puffy," Robert Q answered. "I didn't do anything. We were taking a walk and the next thing I knew, Gerrie sort of. . . . yelped, and then she fell. I think something hit her. On the head. From behind."

"Something?" someone said. Hailey heard skepticism in the voice. She also recognized it. It was the same voice that had asked her, earlier that evening in the kitchen, if she was sick. Finn Conran's voice.

She saw him moving forward in the crowd.

He was tall, and his head bumped one of several dozen glowing, beer-bottle-shaped plastic lights strung above the lawn. "Like what kind of something?" Finn asked Robert Q.

"How should I know?" Robert Q, still kneeling beside Gerrie's silent form, glanced around. He reached out and picked up an object. "Like this rock, maybe? It's heavy enough to sandbag Gerrie, and that looks like blood on it."

"Ooh, gross!" Puffy squealed.

"Who else was out here?" Finn asked Robert Q.

"No one. Just us. Someone must have been hiding."

"Who would want to hurt Gerrie?" Susan Grossbeck wailed.

Are you kidding? Hailey thought. Everyone Gerrie had ever snubbed, which probably included at least half the campus. But then the feeling of doom returned as Hailey realized that tonight one person had plenty of reason to throw a rock at Gerrie Northrup: Darlene Riggs. Who had a better motive than Darlene?

Lindsey Kite had exactly the same thought. "That *townie*," she said in a loud voice. "That Darlene. Just before she left the living room, she gave Gerrie a look that positively gave me *chills*. *She* could have been hiding out here."

Hailey remembered the look in Darlene's eyes when she left, and said nothing.

As a siren sounded in the distance, Gerrie stirred and moaned.

"Oh, thank God!" Puffy sang out, "She's alive! Gerrie's alive!"

By the time the paramedics arrived, Gerrie was conscious but disoriented, complaining that her vision was blurred. Robert Q accompanied her in the ambulance, although he made it clear right up until the doors closed that he wasn't at all happy about leaving while Sigma Chi was hosting a party. He was especially worried about his car.

"Keep an eye on my Miata," he ordered Richard Wentworth as the ambulance doors swung shut. "Don't let anyone *near* it! We don't even *know* some of these people." He was referring to the party guests, many of whom weren't members of Sigma Chi.

"What a guy," Finn said to Hailey as the crowd, murmuring among themselves, dispersed. "Anyone could see he's worried sick about that girl."

Hailey grimaced. "Yeah, must be true love."

"Listen," Finn said, "do you really want to go back inside?"

"No." She smiled at him. "Got a better idea?"

"Coffee at the diner. Sound good?"

Hailey's earlier uneasiness returned. The diner would remind her of Darlene. Could Darlene really have thrown the rock that sent Gerrie Northrup away in a shrieking ambulance?

She didn't want to think about that now.

Finn picked up on her lack of enthusiasm. "How about Vinnie's?" he asked, referring to a favorite Italian restaurant not far from campus. "Their coffee is almost as good as their pizza. The only thing is," he added quickly, "I don't have wheels. Any chance you feel like a walk?"

"I have my car," Hailey answered, "but I would like to walk. Of course," she added, grinning, "I will absolutely have to find someone to keep an eye on my precious old secondhand Ford. Maybe Richard Wentworth could do double duty?"

Finn laughed.

During the walk to Vinnie's and while they sipped the strong, hot coffee, they carefully avoided mentioning Gerrie Northrup.

But Hailey could see in Finn's eyes that he was thinking the same thing she was. And she knew they had to talk about it.

"So, do you think it could have been an accident?" she asked, finally.

"I might have thought it was just a stupid prank if Robert Q had seen someone else hanging around out there. But he didn't. Which probably means someone was hiding."

"But," Hailey responded with false hope, "it *could* have been a joke, couldn't it? Maybe someone intending to just rattle the two of them? I mean, maybe the rock or whatever it was, was aimed at one of the plastic lanterns and hit Gerrie instead."

Finn raised a skeptical eyebrow. "Sure. And maybe Robert Q has a heart of gold."

Then two carloads of Sigma Chi partygoers descended on Vinnie's and the place became so noisy Hailey and Finn decided to leave. The newcomers were, of course, gossiping wildly about what had happened to Gerrie, and Hailey didn't want to hear it. Sooner or later, someone would mention Darlene. She *definitely* didn't want to hear that.

Back on campus, Finn walked her to her car. "Can I give you a ride somewhere?" Hailey asked as she slid into the driver's seat. He had told her very little about himself. She'd done most of the talking. She didn't even know where he lived.

"No, thanks." He leaned his arm on the windowsill. "It's just a short walk."

"You're not in a frat house, are you?" She hoped not. That would give him too much in common with Robert Q.

"Nope." He shook his head. "Frats aren't my thing."

She'd bet anything Sigma Chi had wanted him, though. Who wouldn't? She liked that he'd turned them down, and she liked that he wasn't a snob like Robert Q and his crowd.

"See you around," he said, moving away from the car door. "You're at Devereaux, right?"

Had he *asked* someone? About *her*? That was a good sign, wasn't it? She nodded. "Call me," she said impulsively. "I can actually hear the phone ring if my roommate isn't playing the stereo loud enough to shatter glass."

Finn laughed. "I'll let it ring a long time," he said, and then he turned away and broke into a loping gait, headed across campus.

She liked the way he moved, light and easy on his feet.

When Hailey got back to her own dorm, it was quiet. Nell was sound asleep, her face half-covered by her pillow.

Hailey was disappointed. She needed to talk about tonight, about Finn, about what had happened at the party. Nell was so . . . grounded. Hailey's mother would have said "Nell has a good head on her shoulders." It was probably all those years of discipline and training to be a gymnast. Nell might come up with a sensible explanation for Gerrie's "accident" that didn't involve Darlene.

And that was what Hailey wanted. She didn't want Darlene involved in that pool of blood on Sigma Chi's back lawn.

But who *else* had reason to be *that* angry with Gerrie Northrup?

Bo. Bo Jessup, Darlene's ex-boyfriend. *He* had been that angry. He'd made threats. Could he have taken Darlene home and come back to the party? If it *was* Bo, the rock had probably been aimed at Robert Q, and Gerrie had somehow got in the way.

Hailey glanced at her illuminated clock radio. Was it too late to call Darlene? And what, exactly, would she *say*? "Darlene, this is Hailey. I was just wondering if you hid behind a tree tonight at Sigma Chi and threw the rock that bashed in Gerrie's Northrup's skull?"

And what could Darlene say to that? "Yes, I did it and I'm glad"? Or, "Hailey, how could you *think* I would do such an awful thing"? Or, maybe, "It wasn't me. It was Bo."

And if she does deny knowing about the rock-throwing, Hailey asked herself as she slid into bed, will I believe her?

Hailey dreamed that night that she was standing beside the fountain in the center of the commons, watching in horror as a frenzied crowd threw rocks and stones at Darlene, who was trying to shield her face with her hands and crying out for Hailey to help her. But Hailey was frozen to the spot, her limbs paralyzed, unable even to speak.

She awoke early the next morning in a cold sweat. The feeling of impending doom clung to her.

When she had filled Nell in on all the gory details of the Sigma Chi party, she was disappointed by her roommate's reaction.

"Well, Gerrie isn't *dead*, is she?" Nell asked, slipping into gray sweat pants and a matching sweatshirt for her morning run. "So she's got a headache for a few days. She *is* a headache, so don't expect me to crumble in sympathy over Gerrie Northrup."

"That's not the *point*," Hailey argued. "She was probably *attacked*, Nell. On *purpose*. Right here on campus. Doesn't that *bother* you?"

"No." Nell slid a sweatband under her dark bangs. "You and I don't act like Gerrie, pushing people around, treating everyone like dirt, so why should we worry? She made an enemy, that's all. We don't *make* enemies."

Although she had a valid point, Hailey wondered if Nell was deliberately avoiding mentioning Darlene's name. Nell hadn't been at the

44

party, hadn't seen Robert Q and Gerrie welded together, hadn't watched Darlene's face twist in rage. But . . . I *told* her all that, Hailey thought as Nell headed for the door. So she has to know Darlene is the most obvious suspect. Darlene or her ex-boyfriend.

Nell left for her usual thirty-minute run, although the sky outside their window was charcoal gray and they could hear the distant angry rumblings of thunder.

Hailey, telling herself that the feeling of uneasiness she couldn't shake had nothing to do with Nell, headed for the bathroom to take a shower.

Ninety minutes later, Nell still hadn't returned.

# Chapter 6

Hailey didn't know what to do about Nell, who should have returned to the room long ago. She never ran for more than half an hour, and she was missing her nine o'clock class. Nell wouldn't cut a class. She had to keep her grades up to stay on the gymnastics team.

Hailey paced back and forth in the small room. Outside, the rumble of thunder intensified. It was going to storm.

Hailey's earliest Monday class wasn't until ten o'clock. She decided to go look for Nell. She knew Nell's usual route. If she didn't find her, she'd. . . . what? Get help? Call someone? Start a campus search? What *did* you do when someone was . . . missing?

Was Nell *missing*?

Why would Nell be missing?

Refusing to dwell on the worst possible scenario, Hailey threw a yellow, waterproof windbreaker over her T-shirt and jeans, scribbled a quick note to Nell in case she returned before Hailey did, and hurried from the room.

As she followed Nell's run route, Hailey's mind whirled: If Gerrie hadn't been hurt at the party last night, would I be this frantic about Nell? If I didn't have this stupid feeling that something awful was about to happen, would I be chasing after my roommate, when any second now, the skies are going to open up and I'm going to get drenched?

All she could think was that Nell might be lying in the woods somewhere with her head split open like a ripe melon, just like Gerrie. Why did Nell have to run, anyway? None of the other gymnasts ran. Too risky. Tripping over an unseen rock or a fallen tree limb could keep you off the team for weeks with an ace bandage wrapped around your leg.

But Nell had been running regularly since she was eleven, and she refused to give it up. "It clears the morning cobwebs out of my head," she'd told Hailey. "Without it, I'd be a zombie until noon."

Where *was* Nell?

Campus was very quiet. Some people were attending nine o'clock classes, but most were probably still sleeping, Hailey thought. Dark clouds hung low over the wooded area she was aiming for. As she hurried her steps, a few raindrops splattered against her windbreaker, telling her she wasn't going to beat the storm. Hailey tightened her lips and kept going. Wasn't finding her roommate worth getting a little wet?

She was about to step onto the curving dirt path leading into the woods when she heard someone calling her name. She turned to see Nell waving at her from the steps of the science building.

Relief washed over Hailey just as the storm did the same. She was soaking wet in seconds, although she ran as fast as she could to join Nell, who grabbed Hailey's elbow and pulled her inside, out of the downpour.

"Where on *earth* have you *been*?" Hailey gasped, shedding her sodden windbreaker and wiping her face with a tissue she unearthed from her jeans pocket. "You never came back from your run! I was worried sick!"

"Worried? What for?" Nell peered into Hailey's face. "Hailey, what's wrong with you? Why are you so upset?"

"What's wrong with *me*?" Hailey's voice echoed in the huge, empty front hall of the science building. "Nell, you didn't come *back*! What was I supposed to think? You *always* come back in half an hour."

Nell smiled tentatively. "Well, not *always*," she said, a devilish grin in her dark eyes. "I mean, if I *always* came back in half an hour, we wouldn't be having this conversation, would we?" When Hailey failed to return the smile, Nell got serious. "Look, Hailey, I'm sorry you were worried, but I really don't get it. I mean, what did you think had happened?"

"That's just it," Hailey said, exasperated by Nell's attitude, "I didn't *know*."

"So you imagined all kinds of things, right?" Nell leaned against a large glass case containing Salem University's collection of science awards. "Don't you think maybe you overreacted, just a little? I *can* take care of myself, Hailey."

"I'm sure that's exactly what Gerrie Northrup thought yesterday before her brains were bashed in," Hailey cried.

Enlightenment dawned in Nell's eyes. "Oh, Hailey, I'm sorry," she said. "You're still upset about that awful business last night and you thought something like that had happened to *me*?"

Hailey nodded silently. Embarrassment began to overcome her anger. Nell was right: she *had* overreacted. "Where *were* you?" she asked in a calmer voice. "If you hadn't spotted me going into the woods, I'd be in there *now*, in this storm, hunting for you. Why *didn't* you come back to the room?"

Nell sighed. "Because I ran into Darlene and had to listen to her tale of woe for forty-five minutes. I knew if I went back to the room, I'd miss my nine o'clock. So I went straight to class." Nell glanced down at her sweatsuit and made a face of distaste. "Like *this*, I went to class! You should have seen the look on Lindsey Kite's face. Like she'd just smelled something rotten." Nell laughed. "I should dress like this more often. Anyway, Hailey, I'm really sorry. I'd just left class when I saw you heading for the woods. Aren't you missing your ten o'clock?"

Hailey waved a hand in dismissal. A horrendous clap of thunder shook the old building. When it had died, she said, "Doesn't matter. I'll borrow the notes from Jess. What did Darlene want?"

"She's really mad, Hailey. About the Sigma party. She said people couldn't treat her that way and get away with it. And then she went on and on about how some people don't know when to let go, meaning Gerrie, which is weird, since everyone knows it's really *Gerrie* Robert Q wants, and not Darlene. And what's even weirder is that she's mad at everyone *but* Robert Q."

"She *was* mad at him."

"Well, she isn't now." Nell and Hailey moved to the wide, glass-windowed front door to watch the storm. "You know," Nell continued, "Darlene never once asked me if Gerrie was okay. And she'd heard what happened. She said her brother told her. She said people on campus had been looking at her funny, as if she'd done something terrible. I didn't tell her that's *exactly* what everyone thinks. But Hailey, she never once asked me how Gerrie *was*. Don't you think that's pretty weird?"

"Bo wasn't with her, was he? Big guy, dark hair?"

"No. She was alone."

"And she was looking for Robert Q?"

"Yep. She's not going to let go of him, is she?"

"Doesn't look that way."

When Hailey returned from classes later that day, the phone was ringing. When she answered, Darlene's voice said impatiently, "Hailey, is that you? Have you seen Robert Q today?"

"No, Darlene," Hailey answered truthfully, wishing she hadn't picked up the telephone. "I haven't. You didn't run into him on campus?"

"No. But I ran into that snotty Richard Wentworth. He told me Robert didn't want to talk to me. But I know he was lying. He's never liked me, Hailey."

The rumor on campus was that Gerrie Northrup was having serious vision problems as a result of the rock-throwing incident. Hailey had found the news very disturbing. She wasn't a member of the Gerrie Northrup fan club, but she wouldn't wish blindness on even her worst enemy.

"*None* of them ever liked me, Hailey," Darlene was saying. "I should have known it was *their* fault Robert Q asked Gerrie to dance. *They* talked him into it. I'm sure of it."

So that was why she wasn't mad at Robert Q anymore. She'd rewritten the script of the party night. And she'd completely left out the scene where Robert Q bribed Richard into taking Darlene home.

"Darlene," Hailey said, "maybe you should give up on Robert Q. Maybe you could make up with Bo now. He must care for you a lot or he wouldn't have been so upset last night."

"Hailey! I *love* Robert Q. And I know he loves me. He *said* so. Anyway," Darlene deftly switched the subject, "I'm having a pizza party at my house tonight. It'll take everyone's mind off what happened to Gerrie."

Hailey was too shocked to comment. Darlene was planning a party? A *party*? After everything that had happened last night?

"You'll come, won't you, Hailey? And bring Nell. The more, the merrier. My parents will be out, and my brother is going to a swim meet, so we'll have the house all to ourselves. There'll be plenty of room, no matter how big the crowd gets."

"I don't think — " Hailey began, but Darlene interrupted.

"I hope I can get in touch with Robert Q," she said. "He'll bring guys for all the girls. Then I have to call the Omega house and invite Puffy and everyone. And I'd better check with Vinnie and make sure he can handle pizza for so many people. See you tonight, Hailey. Around eight, I think. It's 1006 Fourth Street. 'Bye."

The phone clicked and fell silent before Hailey could say, "Darlene, *no one* will *come*. Especially not Robert Q."


"Is she *crazy*?" Nell cried when Hailey told her about the invitation. "After last night? Everyone thinks she *did* it, Hailey." She tossed her backpack on the bed. "Even if they didn't suspect her, does she really think anyone from Omega house is going to show up at a townie's party?"

"They might," Hailey said without conviction. "They might like the idea of slumming, just for kicks. I can see Puffy going and then making snide remarks about Darlene's party afterwards."

"That sounds like Puffy," Nell agreed. "But she won't go now, not with Gerrie in the hospital. And I don't think anyone else will, either."

"Well, *I'm* going," Hailey said grimly. "I think Darlene's getting a really raw deal from Robert Q and his airhead friends. Are you coming?"

"Can't." Nell saw the expression on Hailey's face. "Honest, Hailey, I *can't!* I've got a paper due tomorrow and an early practice session tomorrow morning. Darlene should have waited till Friday night to have her pizza party. Hardly anyone has Saturday classes. Besides, maybe Gerrie will be out of the hospital by then and one or two people who've forgiven Darlene would actually show up."

"Well, she isn't *having* it Friday night," Hailey said tartly. "She's having it tonight. And *I'm* going. I don't care if I'm the only one there."

Because she had a paper of her own to finish, Hailey didn't leave the dorm until eight-thirty. But it took only ten minutes to drive to town. The diner's parking lot, when she passed it, was full, as was Vinnie's. Hailey couldn't help wishing she were on her way to either of those places instead of Darlene's. Either one would probably be more fun.

The lighted white church spire rising above town pointed the way to Twin Falls. A nearly full moon turned to rippling silver the river that snaked through town.

The huge brick houses lining the left side of Pennsylvania Avenue as Hailey entered town had an unobstructed view of the river and the big park along its opposite bank, now that the giant maple trees lining the avenue had lost their leaves.

At the wide stone bridge spanning the water, Hailey stopped at a traffic light. Downtown was deserted but for a few patrons entering or leaving a pair of restaurants flanking the tall, narrow brick bank building. Mannequins stared, unseeing, from lighted store windows. The few short blocks making up the Twin Falls commercial district, thriving during the day, had, Hailey decided, an eerie quality about them at night, as if all the people had just disappeared.

When she reached Darlene's small, two-story gray house on a street crammed with rows of identical houses, she noticed there were no other cars in the driveway or parked at the curb. And as Hailey rang the doorbell on the porch, she wondered with a sinking heart if she really might be the only party guest.

Darlene opened the door. The first thing Hailey noticed was the look of hope on her face, a look that vanished when she saw Hailey standing alone on the porch. The second thing she noticed was Darlene's outfit. Instead of just jeans and a sweater, Darlene was wearing a hot-pink off-the-shoulder dress. She ushered Hailey into the living room. It was decorated with hanging balloons and draped streamers like, Hailey thought, a fourth-grader's birthday party. The smell of pizza hung heavy in the air.

She went to all this trouble for Robert Q, Hailey thought, feeling sick, and he didn't even bother to come. And if Robert Q and his friends *had* come, they would have laughed at Darlene's dress, and her decorations.

Darlene turned to face Hailey. "They're not coming, are they?" she asked in a low, tight voice. "Not even Robert Q. Am I right?"

In a room that was almost too warm, Hailey felt a chill.

Because although Darlene spoke quietly, her dark brown eyes were full of rage.

# Chapter 7

"I called Sigma Chi," said Darlene, her voice now as cold as her eyes. "The guy who answered told me Robert Q wasn't there." She laughed harshly. "Did he really think I couldn't tell he was lying? How stupid do they think I *am*?"

Hailey didn't have to tell Darlene that everyone at Sigma Chi probably had strict orders from Robert Q himself to tell "the townie" he wasn't available. The expression on Darlene's face said she already knew that.

Without another word, Darlene suddenly whirled and raced out of the room. She ran back in a moment later, waving something in the air. "This is Robert Q's tennis letter jacket," she said, her brown eyes glittering like marbles. "He loaned it to me one night when we went to a movie. It was cold in the theater. I thought it was such a sweet thing to do. When he didn't ask for it back, I figured he wanted me to keep it." She began gently stroking the jacket, her eyes dreamy.

Then her expression changed again. The dreamy look disappeared and her mouth tightened. Still holding the jacket, she grabbed Hailey's hand and pulled her into the kitchen, where a pile of large, flat white boxes sat on the counter. "Eight, count them, *eight* large pizzas!" Darlene said bitterly. "I don't know about you, Hailey, but I've never been hungry enough in my life to eat that much pizza!"

Hailey stood awkwardly in the center of the kitchen, feeling confused. She couldn't tell if Darlene was furious or heartbroken. She had no idea what to say to calm her down.

They noticed the knife at precisely the same moment. It was very long and very wide. It lay beside the pizza boxes.

And before Hailey could stop her, Darlene ran to the counter, grabbed the knife, and began slashing wildly at the jacket, crying aloud, "He said he *loved* me! Not her, not Gerrie, *me!*" Tears of rage washed her face as she lifted her arm high in the air to deliver each new slash.

"Darlene, *stop* it!" Hailey screamed when she found her voice. Thoroughly frightened, she hesitated, afraid of getting in the way of that wickedly slashing knife. But she couldn't simply stand by and *watch*. "*Stop* it!" she screamed again, "calm *down* or . . . or I'm leaving! Put that knife *down*!"

Darlene stopped slashing. She lifted her head and looked at Hailey as if she'd forgotten anyone was there. Then she sagged against the counter and let go of the knife. It fell to the floor. Darlene looked down at the ragged remnants of Robert Q's jacket and said in a voice drained of any emotion, "Well, he won't be wearing *this* any time soon, will he?"

Shaking, Hailey walked over and picked up the knife. She stuck it in a drawer before returning to Darlene.

"I don't suppose you feel like eating any pizza now, do you?" Darlene asked. Her cheeks were streaked with mascara, her face very pale.

Taking Darlene's arm, Hailey led her to a stool in front of the counter, and then took another stool for herself.

Darlene sat placidly, her hands in her lap.

Watching her, Hailey found it hard to believe that only moments earlier, the girl opposite her had been wild with rage.

"Darlene," Hailey finally said quietly, "are you okay?"

And Darlene turned to her with a face serenely composed. She smiled sweetly. "Of course, Hailey. I don't know what got into me.

I'm sorry if I scared you." Then, a moment later, Darlene said, "I can't believe I was mad at Robert Q. It's *so* obvious that none of this is his fault. I'm sure that jerk at Sigma Chi never even told him I called."

Hailey shifted uncomfortably on her stool. Was this the same person who had gone wild with a knife just minutes ago?

"Hailey, don't look so worried. I'm fine, honest. But," she said, swivelling on the stool, "you know, I really need to talk to Robert Q. Would you mind if we cut this party short?"

Hailey was only too willing to leave. But she couldn't go without saying something about Robert Q. "Darlene," she began hesitantly as she slid off her stool, "maybe Robert Q just isn't the guy for you. I mean, look what this is doing to you! Don't you think you'd be happier — "

Darlene interrupted. "Forget Robert Q? Why would I want to do that? We *love* each other, Hailey."

Hailey gave up. It was hopeless. One minute, Darlene was shredding Robert Q's jacket, and the next minute she *loved* him. Hopeless.

Darlene's voice hardened again. "I don't intend to be a waitress for the rest of my life, Hailey. Just because I didn't get a college scholarship to Salem like my brother, people shouldn't think I'm stupid." She smiled coldly. "Thinking I'm stupid would be a mistake. A *big* mistake."

Then she began complaining again about Gerrie Northrup and Robert Q's other friends. Hailey tuned out, and began edging her way toward the front door. Darlene's invective became more and more heated, and Hailey was enormously relieved when the tirade was interrupted by the arrival of Darlene's parents.

Darlene's mother looked exactly like an older Darlene. Her father was a small, quiet, tired-looking man. Hailey admired the couple for the way they hid their shock at seeing only one guest and enough leftover pizza to feed their family for days.

When Hailey left, Mrs. Riggs said warmly, "Thank you for coming, Hailey. Please come again."

*She knows,* Hailey told herself as she drove away. *I saw it in her eyes. She knows exactly what's happening and she doesn't know how to help Darlene.*

*Join the club, Mrs. Riggs,* she thought grimly. *I don't know how to help your daughter, either.*

When she reached campus, Hailey went straight to the library to finish up the bibliography for her English paper. She glanced around the huge first floor, hoping to see Finn. When she didn't see him, she took a seat near the wide front windows. Seeing Darlene's strange behavior had bothered her more than she wanted to admit. And she couldn't shake an unsettling feeling that something terrible was going to happen.

At closing time, an hour or so later, Hailey was preparing to leave when, through the window, she saw people running past the library. It was obvious, even by the faint light from lampposts on either side of the library entrance, that they weren't out for an evening jog. They were *running*. *Toward* something? Hailey wondered, grabbing her books, or . . . *from* something? The feeling of dread descended upon her again as she hurried outside.

They were running *toward* something, she discovered as she and a few other library stragglers reached the wide stone steps. A fat, black plume of smoke snaked its way toward the dark night sky from . . . behind the Sigma Chi house. Hailey could hear shouting in the distance, and the faint wail of a siren approaching from town.

Fire!

Hailey's heart began to pound as her feet joined the thudding of other feet racing toward the fraternity house.

The group followed the plume of smoke to

its source, the parking lot behind the big brick frat house. A crowd had already gathered in a semicircle a safe distance from the blaze. Which, to Hailey's relief, was *not* the house.

A car was on fire. Unrecognizable now, it was a solid mass of red, orange, and yellow flames. The smell of burning leather was sickening. A figure illuminated by the blaze was hopping around the inferno, waving its arms and shouting indiscernable words.

"That's Robert Q," a voice behind Hailey said, the words tinged with disbelief. "That's *his* Miata!"

Hailey looked at the figure again. Robert Q? This madman in shorts and T-shirt and barefoot, his hair sticking up every which way, features distorted with rage, was the impeccably dressed and groomed, unflappable Mr. Smooth?

"Interesting dance he's doing," a deep voice said into Hailey's left ear.

She turned to find Finn standing beside her. In the flame-brightened darkness, she could see amusement in his eyes.

"What happened?" she asked him. "How did it start?"

"Beats me. I just got here."

"*She* did it!" Susan Grossbeck's voice rang out as she pushed her way to the front of the crowd. "I saw her on campus this morning, hunting for Robert Q. The poor guy was hiding from her all day."

"Who are you talking about, Susan?" Hailey asked cooly, although she knew the answer.

"Darlene! She must have been really ticked off when she couldn't find Robert. Then she asked us all to her stupid pizza party. Of *course* we didn't go. Why *would* we? That must have made her even madder. So she came up here and deliberately set Robert Q's car on fire. She should be arrested!"

"Or sent to one of those places for the criminally insane," Puffy, standing beside Susan, agreed.

Hailey remembered the rage in Darlene's eyes. And Darlene had had plenty of time to make the trip to campus while Hailey was in the library.

Her stomach churning, Hailey returned her attention to Robert Q. His crazy hip-hopping dance *was* comical, she decided, and allowed a small smile to slide across her face. After all, it wasn't as if anyone had been hurt in the fire.

The fire truck arrived. In minutes, Robert Q's little red sportscar became a heap of charred, smoldering metal. He stood in a puddle of water, staring bleakly at the remains, looking as if he might burst into tears at any moment.

Then Susan wailed, "Poor Robert Q's hands are burned! They look awful, all red and scorched, like boiled lobsters."

In an undertone, Finn said to Hailey, "That's because the idiot grabbed the door handles when he first got here. I saw him. He was yelling something about a suede jacket inside the car. Everyone warned him not to touch the doors, but you know Robert Q. Doesn't listen to anyone. Those door handles had to be red-hot. No wonder he screamed. He'll feel *that* for a while."

"He'll have new wheels within twenty-four hours," someone said. "Robert Q Parker the second will see to that."

The excitement over, the crowd began to thin. Pete Torrance came over to ask Finn and Hailey if they'd heard what started the fire.

When they said no, he told them a fire fighter had said the fire looked like arson.

They had begun walking away from the scene. Hailey stopped in her tracks. "You mean, someone deliberately set Robert Q's car on fire?" She was remembering Susan's accusation about Darlene.

"Why does that surprise you?" Pete asked. "Don't you think there are people on this campus who rejoiced tonight to see Robert Q losing his cool?"

"Of course. Sure there are. Lots of them, I guess. But starting a fire on purpose . . ." Hailey's voice faded as a shudder of fear swept through her. "I thought it was probably a defective engine or something."

Then Pete began talking to someone else. Hailey and Finn began walking again, across a campus well-lit by old-fashioned round globes on tall metal poles. She told him about Darlene's party, and how she'd been the only guest. She didn't mention how Darlene had attacked Robert Q's jacket, though.

At Lester Dorm, Finn told Hailey good night. But as he turned to leave, he hesitated and then whirled around and said, "Listen, I think the way you care about Darlene is really great. She's lucky to have someone like you on her side." He smiled. "I wouldn't mind getting that lucky."

Startled, Hailey stammered, "Oh, well, thanks. Darlene may not be perfect, but she doesn't deserve to be stepped on."

"Right. Well, see you," he said, and Hailey turned and left.

The acrid smell of smoke hung in the night air as Hailey returned to her dorm, wondering who, besides Darlene, hated Robert Q enough to deliberately destroy the only thing he seemed to care about.

# Chapter 8

Darlene called Hailey early the next morning. Still in her white terrycloth robe, Hailey sighed when she recognized the voice. It was too early in the morning for any heavy-duty conversation. Communicating required too much brain power from someone who was basically a night person and couldn't even match a pair of socks until she'd had her coffee.

But Darlene was already expressing her shock over the loss of Robert Q's car, and his scalded hands. "I tried to call him, the minute Mike told me about it."

"Mike?"

"My brother. He was on campus last night. He saw the whole thing. He heard that the fire chief thinks someone set fire to the fuel line. Robert Q must be devastated!"

"I guess you could call it that," Hailey agreed, leaning against the wall. Fellow dorm residents wandered sleepily back and forth in the hall, a towel or cup of coffee in hand. Music drifted from more than one room and the sharp clickety-click of an old typewriter set Hailey's teeth on edge . . . too jarring a sound for so early in the morning. "So," she asked Darlene, "did you talk to Robert Q?"

"No, not yet. Thanks to those creeps at Sigma Chi." A heavy sigh came over the wire. "I guess I shouldn't have followed Robert Q yesterday. Dumb idea. I wasn't thinking."

"Oh, Darlene, you didn't! I thought Susan and Puffy were making that up. You really *followed* Robert Q?"

"I *said* it was dumb, didn't I?" Darlene snapped. "I won't make a mistake like that again. Listen, Hailey, I called to tell you I have to go to my grandmother's for a few days. She's got pneumonia. My parents want one of us to go with them. Mike can't miss any classes, so I've been elected. My grandmother lives in Willowcreek, about two hours from here. But we're leaving in half an hour and since I can't get in touch with Robert Q, I'll give you my grandmother's number. Will you give it to him? And tell him why I had to leave?"

Hailey had no intention of delivering a message that would either be shrugged off, or worse, laughed at. To avoid a lie, she said, "I'm sorry about your grandmother, Darlene. I hope she gets better fast. Call me when you get back."

But Darlene was not so easily dismissed. "You'll tell Robert Q? That I had to go out of town?"

Why? Hailey thought. He doesn't *care*. Aloud, she said, "Don't worry about Robert Q, Darlene." But she jotted down the number on a piece of paper before she said good-bye.

Hailey replaced the receiver with an enormous sense of relief. Darlene was leaving town. Maybe, away from Robert Q, she'd have a clearer view of all his character flaws. Hailey smiled to herself. There were so *many*. Maybe Darlene would meet some nice, cute guy in Willowcreek, someone who wouldn't treat her like something to wipe his feet on.

But her smile disappeared as a more sobering thought struck her. Not once during the disastrous pizza party or during their telephone conversation just now had Darlene asked how Gerrie Northrup was doing. Not, "Is she okay?" Not, "Is she going to be permanently blind?" Nothing. Not a word about Gerrie.

Hailey lay on her bed, her eyes focused on the photo hanging over her bed. It was her graduation picture, a colored photograph of her in cap and gown. She was smiling in the picture, and triumphantly waving her diploma. Her hair had behaved that day, so it was a better-than-usual likeness of Hailey Court Kingman. And to her, it was also a photograph of both an ending *and* a beginning. Looking at the picture made her feel good, so she had put it where she could look at it often.

Nell was not as sentimental. They had argued, that first week, over what Nell chose to hang on *her* wall. She had tacked a poster over her bed. Although Hailey found it disturbing, the ecologically conscious Nell refused to take it down. "It's about something important, Hailey," she had said, and the poster remained in place.

The giant photo depicted a huge mountain of trash: empty cans, bottles, jars, newspapers, magazines, clothing, disposable diapers, household appliances, furniture, and countless stuffed plastic bags, many split open, spilling their contents. Printed in large block letters under the picture was the question, *IS THIS ANY WAY TO TREAT A PLANET?* And under the question was the commandment: *RECYCLE!*

Hailey thought the poster was ugly, even scary. But Nell had said, "That's the whole point. It's *supposed* to be repulsive. That way, maybe people who look at it will think twice about tossing their sixty-four ounce plastic soda bottles in the trash."

Hailey stared at the disturbing poster, thinking, That must be pretty much the way my mind looks right about now. There's so much going on, and I can't sort it all out.

According to her radio, a rare, early cold front had invaded the area during the night. Hailey dressed in a heavy green sweater, jeans, and boots, still thinking about her conversation with Darlene.

Why hadn't Darlene asked about Gerrie?

Was it because Darlene really *had* thrown that rock?

Hailey bent to tie the laces on her boots. The image of Darlene slashing at Robert Q's jacket flashed in her head. Was Darlene's grandmother really sick? Or was Darlene suddenly anxious to leave Twin Falls because she was afraid the police might want to ask her some questions, about Gerrie *and* about the fire that destroyed Robert Q's car?

Who had a better motive than Darlene Riggs to throw the rock and set the fire?

Well, Bo Jessup, for one. He *had* to hate Robert Q.

The thing to do, Hailey told herself, cramming her thick strawberry-blonde hair under a floppy brown felt hat, is wait and see what happens now, with Darlene two hours away in Willowcreek.

As she hurried across campus fighting a brisk northerly wind smelling of snow to come, Hailey spotted Robert Q, his hands bandaged in white. He was flanked by Lyle and Richard. It seemed strange to see them on foot. She was used to Robert Q tooling around campus in the red Miata. She'd seen him hop into it to drive no more than a few hundred yards from building to building on campus. Lyle, Hailey had heard, had had his license suspended for drinking while driving, and Richard's father had refused to let his son bring a car to campus until he had "proved himself" academically. Now that Robert Q's car had been reduced to melted metal, the trio had no wheels at all.

They looked like little boys whose favorite toy had been confiscated.

But, as someone had said the night before, Robert Q would probably have new wheels before the sun set. And he'd find a way to drive in spite of the white mittens on his hands. Then they'd all be smiling again.

She hurried past them without a greeting, and when one of them — Richard, she thought — called her name, she pretended she hadn't heard. They'd ask her about Darlene, and no way was she discussing Darlene with those three.

But, as she quickly discovered throughout the day, Darlene was the subject *du jour*. The topic of the day. No one wanted to talk about anything else. Darlene, it was said, was a woman scorned, wild with fury at both Robert Q and Gerrie, and had therefore punished both of them.

"I heard," Puffy told a group shivering out on the commons at noon, "that the police went to her house this morning to question her, and she wasn't there. She's skipped town!"

Hailey, hurrying home, couldn't help remembering that the same thought had crossed *her* mind. She was tempted to stop and find out more about what the police had done, but she was freezing. The temperature had plummeted and she hadn't worn gloves. Her fingers felt like ice. Thoughts of her warm, cozy room propelled her feet onward, past the gossiping group.

She was disappointed that she hadn't seen Finn Conran all day. No wonder the sky looked so black and gloomy. Or was it because campus had become such a scary place to be?

Had the police really gone to Darlene's house? What had they thought when they discovered she'd left town? Was her brother home to explain, or did he live on campus? Darlene hadn't said.

Hailey couldn't really blame the police for wondering about Darlene. Wasn't *she* wondering about Darlene, too?

And *I* know her, she thought guiltily. The police *don't* know her. All they know is that Darlene had a very strong motive for hurting both Gerrie and Robert Q. The oldest motive in the world: jealousy.

But Bo Jessup had a motive, too: revenge. Did the police know about Bo?

It was a relief to be out of the wind, with the heavy front door of Devereaux Hall closed behind her. The building rang inside with dozens of stereos competing with each other, footsteps pounding along six floors of corridors, muted laughter and chatter escaping from behind closed dorm rooms. The elevator hummed behind her as she climbed the stairs to the second floor.

Nell probably wouldn't be home for a little while. She had gymnastics practice every afternoon from two o'clock to four, and it was just four o'clock. Hailey didn't mind being alone. It would be nice, after such a rotten day of nasty gossip, to have the room all to herself. Peace and quiet, that was what she needed.

The door to room 242 wasn't locked. Although the administration and the Devereaux resident advisors had issued strict warnings about everyone locking their doors during that horrible business at Nightingale Hall, Hailey had lost or forgotten her keys so often, Nell had finally thrown up her hands in despair and said, "Okay, okay, so we'll leave the door unlocked! But if some creep comes in here and swipes my stereo, *you're* buying me a new one."

Hailey *did* intend to get a replacement key. It was one of the items on her *TO DO* list push-pinned to the cork bulletin board over her desk. But she hadn't yet made the trip to the campus security office in the administration building.

Maybe tomorrow . . .

Humming softly to herself, Hailey pulled open the door numbered 242.

And stood frozen in horror on the threshold, her mouth open, eyes disbelieving.

In shock, Hailey swayed, and had to lean against the doorframe for support, never taking her eyes off the terrifying scene before her.

All four white walls were streaked with wide slashes of what appeared to be black paint.

The drawers in the twin maple chests had been emptied, their contents dumped out onto the floor. T-shirts, lingerie, jeans, sweatshirts, and sweaters were scattered across the pale blue carpet. Huge, ugly blotches of the same black goo defacing the walls clung to many of the clothing items.

Her beautiful quilt and Nell's bedspread had been sliced to ribbons and tossed haphazardly about the room. A handful of red plaid strips dangled crazily from the brass ceiling fixture in the center of the room.

Both of their bed pillows had been shredded. Fat wads of white foam rubber littered the carpet and polka-dotted the trail of paint-spattered clothing.

The lampshades on two small desk lamps had been pierced so deeply and so repeatedly with something sharp, the light bulbs were clearly visible through the multitude of jagged holes.

Hailey moaned, a sound thick with pain.

Every desk drawer was not only empty, its contents ripped and tossed, but the drawers themselves had been stomped into fragments. Chunks of inexpensive wood lay in corners and under the beds.

The most hideous act of vandalism was so unexpected, so stunning, that at first Hailey couldn't believe what she thought she saw.

But, peering at the grotesque sight more closely, she realized there was nothing wrong with her vision. Her lunch rose into her throat.

What the vandal had done was remove Hailey's graduation photo from its frame, then carefully cut out her figure. Then, slicing a narrow slit in Nell's ugly landfill poster, he had thrust the figure of Hailey, headfirst, into the mountain of trash. The upper part of her body had disappeared behind the poster, making it look as if she had been buried in the mountain. Only the lower half of her body was visible, but she knew who was wearing that blue graduation gown and those black pumps.

The message was clear. Someone wanted Hailey Kingman buried.

# Chapter 9

People passing by in the hall saw Hailey crumpled in a heap in the doorway, and stopped. Like Hailey, they were shocked into silence by the utter devastation in her room. There were only soft whispers of horror as a crowd gathered around her.

"Call security!" a voice commanded, and then a strong arm lifted Hailey and supported her. "I was looking for you." It was Finn. "But I didn't expect to find you in a war zone." He turned her toward him, away from the wreckage. "Are you okay?"

At first, Hailey couldn't speak, or even nod. Then she forced out, "The poster . . . it's so horrible . . ."

"Poster?" Finn leaned around her to glance into the room. He made a sound of disgust low in his throat. "You're right. It's pretty awful.

Look, let's get out of here. Security and maintenance can handle this."

"No. I can't leave. I have to be here when Nell gets back. I can't let her walk in on this." Hailey raised her eyes to meet his. "Why would someone *do* this? *Why?*"

"Why what?" Nell's voice asked as she pushed her way through the crowd to Hailey's side. "What's going on?"

"Don't go *in* there!" Hailey cried sharply, then quickly added more quietly, "Our room's been trashed."

"Trashed?" Nell took a step forward, but Finn blocked her way.

"Hailey's right," he told Nell. "It's not a pretty sight."

"Maybe not. But it's *my* room, and I want to see what's happened to it." Nell darted past Finn and into the room. Her horrified gasp echoed throughout the silent group standing near the door.

Nell appeared in the doorway again, her black eyes snapping with rage. "Who would *do* this?" she cried. "What kind of animal went on a rampage in here?" Then her anger left her and she sagged against the open door. "Oh, Hailey," she said softly, "all our things . . ."

Two uniformed campus security officers appeared, followed by a young man from maintenance. The officers began asking questions of Nell and Hailey. The questions seemed endless. And, for the most part, unanswerable.

But when one of the officers asked Hailey if she had any idea who might have wreaked such havoc, she saw again Darlene wildly slashing at Robert Q's sweater. *That* kind of rage could have destroyed their room, couldn't it?

But Darlene had no reason to be angry with Hailey or Nell. Did she?

"Maybe," Hailey said slowly, "a guy named Bo Jessup. I don't really *know* Bo," she admitted. "I just know that he might be angry with Nell and me, for helping his girlfriend when she was dating someone else." Bo had a temper. He could easily have been angry enough to do some pretty severe damage.

Although the guard shook his head in impatience with the romantic goings-on at the university, he promised to question Bo Jessup.

Their resident advisor, Michelle Chang, arrived. There was, Hailey and Nell were told, an empty room on the fourth floor. Two girls had recently moved into the Tri-Delta house.

But before they could check out the fourth floor, there were reports to be filled out, more questions to go unanswered, and the salvaging of those few objects left untouched by the vandal. Finn stayed with Hailey throughout all of it, leaving only long enough to call Burgers Etc. and explain that he wouldn't be in to work that night.

The crowd of onlookers offered to help the girls uncover the few belongings left intact. Hailey and Nell thanked them, but refused the offer. Neither of them could bear the thought of any more hands touching their things.

Then they learned, to their dismay, that there wouldn't *be* any clean-up just yet. One of the security men told them they wouldn't be able to remove from the premises anything more than a toothbrush until the Twin Falls police had investigated the scene.

"Can we at least," Hailey asked in a shaky voice, "get rid of that horrible poster?" Her eyes avoided the grotesquerie as she pointed sideways.

"Sorry, miss. It'll have to stay for now. Likely to have fingerprints." The middle-aged man in khaki smiled at her with sympathetic eyes. "But soon as the police are done in here, I'll get rid of that for you, I promise."

"Thanks."

Toothbrushes but not much else in hand, Hailey and Nell followed Michelle upstairs to room 416, their new home. As she handed each of them a key, Hailey again thought how stupid they'd been to leave their door unlocked. Then again, judging by the violence of the attack, a locked door wouldn't have stopped him . . . or her. The real question wasn't *how*, but *who*? And *why*?

Who hated Hailey Court Kingman and Ellen Marie Riley enough to commit such a vile act against them? What had they *done* to make someone so angry?

Room 416 was immaculate. The wide windows that cranked outward over the commons were bright, even on such a gray, gloomy day.

Still, in spite of the cheerfulness, the room felt foreign and unwelcoming to Hailey. The white walls were so bare, the built-in dressers free of jars and bottles, hairbrushes and combs and makeup, the bedside tables empty of alarm clocks and magazines, the desks empty of papers and books, the closets holding only naked metal hangers.

"We'll have to start from scratch," she whispered to Nell. "After we worked so hard getting our room just the way we wanted it."

Assuring the two girls that "nothing like this will ever happen again here at Devereaux," Michelle left.

Nell, seeing the despair in Hailey's eyes, said with false bravado, "We'll *make* this room ours, Hailey." Tears moistened her lower lashes.

"And I promise, I won't hang a single poster that you're not crazy about."

As if it were *Nell's* fault that her poster had been used to send an ugly message. "We'll pick out new posters together," Hailey said as cheerfully as she could manage.

And then, unable to keep up the front, she covered her face with her hands and began crying quietly.

Nell did the same.

They sat on one of the beds, crying out their anger and fear and shock until Finn, who had stayed behind to talk to one of the security guards, arrived.

He didn't tell them to stop crying. Instead, he disappeared again and returned a few minutes later to hand each of them a small white towel. "Compliments of the occupants of room 418," he said. "They heard about what happened and were glad to help. Cassie and Joanne. You can thank them in person when you return the towels."

Hailey wiped her eyes with the towel and flashed Finn a grateful smile.

"Now," he said, "if you're really ready to show the world that no crazy vandal is going to send you into hiding, dinner's on me. Well, actually, dinner's on Caesar, my manager at work. When I told him why I wasn't coming in tonight, he insisted we all come there for a free meal. He's one of the good guys. So how about it?"

Although neither girl felt like eating, they were eager to get away from Devereaux Hall and the memory of what room 242, two floors below them, looked like.

"We'd love to go," Hailey said.

They were about to leave when a group of four girls appeared in the open doorway. Two of the girls carried sheets, blankets, and towels. Another girl held a round white wicker basket filled with toothpaste tubes, bars of soap, washcloths, even a curling iron. The fourth girl had her arms laden with looseleaf binders, notebook paper, a package of ballpoint pens, a calendar, several posters, a Salem University pennant, and, on top of the pile, a well-worn paperback dictionary.

"Hi!" the tallest girl said. "I'm Amy. This is Rita," pointing to the white wicker-basketed girl. "We're in 420. And that's Delsey, with the school supplies, and that's Ann, with the towels. They're in 414. We heard what happened, so we collected a few things to tide you over. Welcome to the fourth floor."

Hailey and Nell were so touched, they had to fight against fresh tears. They managed to thank the girls and promised, when requested, to let Amy know if they needed anything else.

When the gift-bearing group had returned to their own rooms, Hailey, Nell, and Finn left for Burgers Etc. Hailey was very careful to lock the door of room 416 as they left.

When they arrived at Burgers Etc., they noticed a brand-new bright yellow Miata in the parking lot. The color made it difficult *not* to notice it.

"That's Robert Q's," Finn said. "Delivered this afternoon at three o'clock. *Less* than twenty-four hours after his old one burned. Papa Parker's a man of action. Not to mention big bucks."

"Darn!" Hailey declared, glaring at the car. "I was hoping Robert Q would have to suffer for at least a *day*."

"Well, I think it's ugly," Nell said. "And Gerrie will hate it."

"She's leaving," Finn said.

"Leaving? Gerrie's leaving campus?"

Finn nodded as they entered the diner. It was warm and noisy inside. "Yeah. She has to have some delicate surgery if she's going to see okay again. Her parents are coming up here next week to take her to Philadelphia for the operation. She won't be riding in Robert Q's new car for a long time, if ever."

As they glanced around, however, it quickly

became clear that, in spite of Gerrie's absence, Robert Q wouldn't be riding alone in the new yellow car. He and Lyle were seated in a large corner booth. Each had an attractive girl seated beside him. The tall, dark-haired girl with Robert Q seemed fascinated with him.

"She is practically," Nell said with disgust, "sitting in his *lap!*"

"A few of Gerrie's friends," Hailey pointed out, "are over there staring daggers at Robert Q. Maybe now they actually see him for the faithless toad he *is*."

"I wonder where Richard Wentworth is," Nell said. "Their booth looks unbalanced without him."

To Hailey, *Darlene's* absence from Burgers Etc. was more noticeable than Gerrie's. The last time they'd been in the diner was the night Darlene had met Robert Q. And now, there he was, busy impressing someone else without a thought for either Gerrie or Darlene.

Hailey picked up her menu. "I wonder if your boss has a side dish featuring arsenic? We could have a complimentary serving sent to Robert Q's table."

When they had made their own selections, Hailey realized they were being stared at. Word of the vandalism had obviously traveled across campus already.

Suddenly she found herself slowly surveying the room with her eyes, studying each table's occupants, looking for . . . what? What did she expect to see? A clue? Some sign that one of the people sharing this warm, comfortable diner with them had entered their room at Devereaux Hall and totally trashed it?

Could you recognize a vandal just by looking at him? What would someone that sick *look* like?

She noticed nothing out of the ordinary. Everything at Burgers Etc. looked the way it always did, as if nothing extraordinary had happened that afternoon. But it *had*. Something horrible had happened, and she knew now that there was someone out there who hated Hailey Kingman. She didn't know who and she wasn't sure why. She only knew that it was so.

# Chapter 10

The next morning, Hailey and Nell were awakened with a start by a knock on their door. Hailey threw on a robe and stumbled over to yank the door open. A security guard stood in the hall.

Disoriented upon waking up in an unfamiliar, barren room, Hailey had trouble understanding what the man wanted.

"I hate to bother you," he said. "But I have to ask you both to come downstairs to your old room and tell us if anything is missing."

"Missing?" Hailey echoed. "Everything is . . . ruined. How could we possibly tell if anything is *missing*? And I don't see what difference it makes."

"The difference," the officer said, "is that when we catch this guy, we'd like to lay as many charges on him as possible. We have a suspect in the car arson, and we think it might be the same guy. So we need all the information from you that we can get."

He wouldn't tell her who the suspect was.

Hailey was disappointed. If she knew, she'd know who to be *afraid* of.

The officer waited in the hall while Hailey and Nell dressed quickly.

Entering room 242 was one of the most painful things Hailey had ever done. Seeing the wreckage a second time was almost as shattering as the first. The room was still a shambles.

"It looks like a bomb exploded in here," Nell murmured. Her eyes were glazed with fresh shock.

Working through the rubble actually helped. Some of the clothes were unmarked by the black paint, which lifted their spirits. And remarkably, Nell's stereo, upside down in a corner, still worked.

"My father said it pays in the long run to buy the best," she told Hailey, "and he was right."

When they had finished sorting through the ruins, they told the security officer that nothing seemed to be missing.

But when they returned to room 416 with

the salvaged clothes, and the officer who had volunteered to carry the stereo had gone, Nell announced, "I lied."

"Lied?" Trying not to think about the wreckage they'd just left, Hailey hung half a dozen shirts in one of the closets.

"I lied to those security guys. There *was* stuff missing."

"What stuff?" Hailey walked to the window to gaze out over the Commons. An unusually early snowfall had arrived during the night. The campus looked so beautiful, so peaceful. "Are you sure? I didn't notice anything missing."

"All our hair stuff. Our brushes, curling irons, mousse, gel, hairdryers, all gone. And our makeup, too. Yours was in that clear plastic thing. Mine was in a peach zippered pouch, remember? They weren't anywhere in the room."

Hailey turned away from the window. The room suddenly seemed very cold. "Our *hair* stuff? Are you sure?"

Nell sat down on her bed. "Well, of *course*, I'm sure. There wasn't so much as a mascara wand in that room. I didn't say anything to the officers because it seemed so silly. I mean, *hair* stuff?" She shivered. "Gives me the creeps. Why would someone take *that*?"

When Hailey said nothing, Nell continued, "Weird, isn't it? Nothing *else* was missing. Not even the pearls my grandmother gave me for my birthday, Hailey. And they're worth a lot of money."

Hailey's knees felt funny. They didn't seem to want to hold her up. "That's all that's missing? The hair things?" She sank to the floor and sat facing Nell. "That's *too* weird," she breathed. "Whoever did it really *does* have a screw missing." Hailey's eyes widened. "Nell, do you remember the last time we used all that stuff? I mean, all of it at the same time?"

Nell thought for a minute. "Sure. We dragged it all out the day Darlene was here."

They looked at each other silently for several seconds.

The horrible image of Darlene's vicious attack on the sweater filled Hailey's mind again. She shook her head to erase the picture.

"Nell, I think we should tell the police what's missing. It *is* a clue. Now that they have a suspect, they need information."

"I wish we knew who it was."

"Me, too."

"You know, Hailey," Nell said thoughtfully, "we *were* the ones who helped Darlene with her hair and makeup. And it didn't *work*. Robert Q dumped her, anyway. Maybe . . . maybe she blames *us*."

Hailey thought about that for a minute. "She didn't *act* like she was mad at me the night of her party. Not at *me*. But . . . she *was* mad." Enraged might be a better word, Hailey thought glumly. "But Darlene couldn't have trashed our room. She's in Willowcreek."

"You mean she *said* she was going to Willowcreek."

"You think she lied?"

"I don't know. But she lies to herself about Robert Q. We really don't *know* Darlene that well, Hailey. Listen, I don't want to talk about this anymore, okay? It's too creepy. I'm still upset about yesterday."

Hailey nodded. Nell was right. They didn't need to borrow trouble by speculating about Darlene. They had enough to handle already. Like, was the sicko who had destroyed their room the same person who had torched Robert Q's car? And was he finished with them now? Or was there more to come if he wasn't arrested soon?

"You're right," Hailey said. "Look, we need to replace all that stuff. Why don't we go to the mall at lunch? I'd really rather crawl into bed and stay there, but we can't live like that, right? We need to do something constructive.

If the roads are a mess, we'll hop the shuttle. You'll be back in time for practice."

Relieved that the discussion was over, Nell agreed to the mall trip.

By noon, although the roads had been plowed, it was snowing again, drawing a thick white curtain across campus.

"We're taking the shuttle," Hailey told Nell when they met at the fountain, shut off for the winter, in the Commons. "The shuttle, like the post office, always operates."

Hailey was delighted to see Finn sitting with Pete on the wide seat at the rear of the small yellow shuttle bus that ran from campus into Twin Falls.

She was *not* pleased to see Robert Q, flanked by Puffy and Lindsey, occupying a middle seat.

"I guess he's not taking any chances with his new toy," Nell said drily. She and Hailey moved down the aisle toward Finn and Pete. "Driving in *this* weather could land his new car upside down in a ditch somewhere."

Mimicking Robert Q's voice, Hailey said, "But *this* car is a miracle of engineering. It can handle *anything*."

"Except an early snowfall, I guess," Nell said, laughing.

Robert Q overheard the exchange. The corners of his lips turned down in annoyance.

"So, where are his sidekicks, Richard and Lyle?" Hailey asked.

Finn explained, "Richard's father finally gave in and let him lease a car to drive. So Richard went out and got the most expensive car he could find. Pig-headed fool that he is, he said he was driving into town today even if it snowed twenty feet. He talked Sutton into going with him."

Thick, wet clumps of snow clung to the shuttle's windows, turning the interior an eerie grayish-yellow.

"They're probably in a ditch somewhere," Nell said. "Serves them right. But why didn't Parker go with them? I never thought of him as sensible."

"He's not," Finn said, pulling up the collar of his jacket. Every time a passenger got on or off the shuttle, a cold wind and blowing snow boarded the bus. "Robert Q had an argument with Lyle and Richard. Everyone on the Commons heard it."

"What about?" Hailey asked, mildly curious. She couldn't imagine those three arguing. They seemed so much alike. All style and no substance, like figures in one of those slick men's magazines. What could they possibly have to argue about?

Finn hesitated. "Nothing. Not important."

But something about the way he said it disturbed Hailey. She turned to look at him. "Finn? *What* did they argue about?"

After another moment's hesitation, he said, "Okay. I guess you'll hear about it, anyway. It was about what happened to your room."

"I heard about that," Pete said. "Nasty deal. You two okay with it now?"

"No, not really," Hailey said coolly. She knew Pete was trying to be nice. But did he really expect them to be "okay" with it? It had happened less than twenty-four hours ago. To Finn, she urged, "Tell us about the argument."

"Robert Q said if you two had minded your own business, your room wouldn't have been trashed. So Lyle and Richard asked him if *he'd* done it."

Hailey shivered in revulsion, picturing Robert Q's hands on her things.

"Well, Robert Q freaked. He shouted at them, said *that* wasn't what he meant, that they were both idiots. Then he said he'd rather *walk* to town than ride with birdbrains. But," Finn grinned, "as you can see, he hopped the shuttle instead."

Hailey sat in silence, staring at the back of Robert Q's head. Why would *he* trash their room?

"Nell," Hailey said quietly, "Robert Q wasn't

the least bit happy when he came to get Darlene in our room that day. Remember?"

"Hailey, I know he's a creep, but do you really think he'd trash our room and steal all our *hair stuff* because we were nice to Darlene? That's crazy!"

"Maybe. But maybe he had a reason we don't know about yet. And it *is* a connection, Nell. Robert Q and Darlene . . ." The idea of someone as cool and controlled as Robert Q wreaking the havoc in their room would once have seemed impossible. But Hailey had *seen* his dance of rage the night his car had burned to a crisp.

Now, it not only seemed possible, it seemed . . . likely.

# Chapter 11

The shuttle dropped Finn and Pete off at the diner, then continued on into town. Robert Q got off, too, telling Puffy and Lindsey he was starving, he wasn't eating "mall food," and he'd catch them later.

At the mall, Hailey and Nell went straight to the drugstore.

It was there that Hailey thought she saw Darlene.

She was trying to decide between two different shades of blusher when she glanced up and saw the top of a curly brown head of hair passing by in the next aisle. The bangs were pinned back by a small brown clip exactly like the one Darlene wore.

Darlene's grandmother must have recovered.

Hailey hurried to the end of the aisle and turned the corner. The brown-haired figure looked back once and then slipped into another aisle.

"Darlene?" Hailey called tentatively.

There was no answer.

Hailey hurried down the aisle and at its end, turned in the same direction taken by the figure. The aisle was empty.

Hailey frowned in annoyance as her eyes scanned the tops of shelves, looking for some sign of the brown curls.

There, over near the toy section! Between tall white doll boxes . . .

"Darlene!" Hailey called again. "Wait!"

The head disappeared.

Hailey broke into a near-run, hurrying toward the shampoo section. She was almost there when a little boy sent a metal shopping cart sailing into her midsection, startling her and knocking the wind out of her. By the time she recovered and rounded a corner, there was no one there.

Feeling foolish, Hailey returned to the hair accessories, unsure if she had actually seen anything at all.

It couldn't have been *Darlene* she'd seen, could it? If Darlene had returned to Twin Falls, she'd have called, wouldn't she?

Hailey took her purchases to the front checkout, where Nell was waiting. As the clerk rang up her items, she thought, I don't *want* Darlene to be back in town. Because if she's here, I'll have to start wondering *when* she got back. *Before* our room was trashed? Or *after*?

"If I don't eat something in the next five minutes," Nell declared as Hailey joined her, "I'm going to embarrass you by collapsing in a heap right here on this brick floor."

Hailey didn't laugh. Why wouldn't Darlene call her if she'd returned to Twin Falls? "The food court is right straight ahead of us. I'm not very hungry, but I guess I should eat."

But all the way there, her eyes scanned the mall for a brunette girl with a brown clip in her hair. It was an exercise in futility. There was no sign of the person she'd spotted in the drugstore.

When they were seated at the food court, Hailey said, "I think we'd better munch fast. When you went hunting for French fries, the guy at the counter told me they might close the mall because of the weather. He said he's worked here for four years and they've never closed it before. So it must be getting pretty nasty out there."

"I *hate* gulping my food," Nell complained. "It's not healthy."

"Nell, you have on your tray two tacos, an order of greasy French fries, and a chocolate sundae. How dare you even *mouth* the word 'healthy'?"

"I'll work all this off at practice. *If*," Nell glanced up at the skylight over their heads, darkened now by a thick layer of white, "we even *have* practice." She brightened visibly. "If classes and practice are canceled, we can spend the rest of the day fixing up our new room."

Mentioning the new room was a mistake. It sobered both girls instantly, reminding them of what had taken place in their "old" room. They ate quickly then, talking only about the weather.

But Hailey found herself nervously checking out each new arrival to the food court, as if by simply looking at people, she could tell whether or not they meant her harm.

She had to force down every bite of food.

Fifteen minutes later, when they exited the mall's main entrance, they were greeted by a thick wall of swirling white. No yellow shuttle bus waited at the curb.

"It'll be late," Nell said as they backed up to share the shelter of the mall's canopy with other waiting, shivering students. "Even if the shuttle has snow tires, visibility is practically zero."

The streetlights in the parking lot were on.

Their faint yellow glow provided little illumination through the blowing snow. But a boy named Tom from Hailey's English class remarked that he could see, over in the parking lot, the car that Richard Wentworth had leased that day. "Right over there," he said, pointing. "The fancy silver job. With the headlights on. Wentworth must be leaving. Anyone feel like hitching a ride to campus with him?"

No one did. The shuttle seemed safer.

Just then, the mall doors opened. Lyle and Richard sauntered out, flanked by Puffy and Lindsey.

"Hey, Wentworth!" Tom called. "Looks like you forgot to turn off your lights. Man, your battery's going to be drained. You'll be shuttling back to campus with the rest of us."

Richard frowned. He peered in the direction of the parking lot. Then he took a few steps forward and said, "That's my car, all right. I had to turn my lights on because of the snow. But I didn't leave them on. I know I turned them off."

Uttering an oath, Richard bolted from the protection of the canopy and began running through the snow toward his car.

It was so hard to see clearly. Later, when the police asked their questions, witnesses to what had taken place had few concrete answers. "We couldn't *see*," they complained.

What Hailey remembered was equally vague, as if the snow curtain had clouded her mind as well as her vision.

Richard had run out into the storm. His bare, blond head had quickly turned snowy-white. As he neared the car with the headlights glowing through the falling snow, he began shouting and waving his arms. It was clear to everyone watching that Richard had not given anyone permission to borrow his new car.

Puffy shrieked, "Someone is stealing it! Someone's stealing Richard's car! Lyle, *do* something!"

Lyle didn't move. "Richard can take care of himself," he said uneasily.

Suddenly, the silver car roared backward, out of its parking space. It skidded briefly, then straightened out and rapidly accelerated to the end of the parking lane, not far from the mall's entrance.

The wind whipped the snow about, making it difficult to see what was going on.

But the group under the canopy could see Richard dash in front of the silver car, waving his arms frantically.

"Is he nuts?" someone cried. Hailey wasn't sure if they were referring to Richard or the driver.

"Wentworth's a fool," Tom said. "He should get out of the way before he gets hurt."

Puffy began screaming, "Richard, get out of the way! Move, Richard, *move!*"

Her voice was lost to the wail of the wind.

And Richard didn't move. He remained stubbornly planted directly in the path of the idling car.

For one brief moment, the wind swept away the white curtain. It was as if the onlookers under the canopy were in a theater and the curtain had been raised so they could see the action on stage.

They all watched in horror as the silver car gunned its engine once, twice, backed up a few feet away from Richard and then, gunning the engine again, sped forward.

The curtain of white closed then, as quickly as it had opened. No one actually saw the impact.

But they *heard* it, in spite of the storm. The thud as metal slammed into flesh was sickening.

Puffy screamed. Several people moaned and sagged against the wall. Others burst into tears at the awful sound, knowing what had happened.

The silver car never stopped. It raced away into the storm.

Richard's body flew up into the air, sailed through the sea of white, and landed only a few feet from the stricken crowd beneath the canopy.

Had he landed on the thick carpet of fluffy snow, Richard Wentworth might have survived.

But he wasn't that lucky. There was a second thud as his body slammed with full force into a huge wooden planter placed to the right of the canopied area. The blowing wind and the protective covering had kept the planter relatively free of what would have been a cushioning blanket of snow. The sickening sound of Richard slamming into the wood was followed instantly by a sharp, cruel crack as his head snapped backward and slammed, a second time, against the unyielding planter.

Then he lay perfectly still, his arms and legs hanging over the edges of the planter, like a broken doll left out in the snowstorm by a careless child.

# Chapter 12

For several seconds after Richard's body slammed into the wooden planter, there was not a sound from the crowd under the canopy. They stood as one, rendered mute by shock and horror.

Then Puffy screamed, a thin, keening sound that snapped everyone back to reality. Lyle ran into the mall to summon help. Tom and another boy rushed to the planter to see if there was anything they could do for Richard.

Hailey held her breath.

But when Tom had checked Richard's pulse, his body language told them it was too late. His shoulders sagged, and he shook his head.

There was nothing anyone could do for Richard now.

Puffy burst into tears, as did several other people. But Lindsey whirled in fury to face Hailey. "*Now* do you believe that girl is crazy?"

White-faced, Hailey stared at her. "*What* girl? What are you talking about?" But she knew exactly who Lindsey was talking about. And she remembered the brown-haired figure in the store. Right *there*, at the mall . . .

"Darlene, of course! First, she hurts Gerrie and burns Robert Q's car. Now she's actually *killed* someone! This is all *your* fault, Hailey. Everyone knows you and Nell encouraged that girl to go after Robert Q. Now she's out to get all of us because you got her hopes up and then he dropped her. She's a maniac, out for revenge! That was *her* in Richard's car. I saw her behind the wheel."

Hailey couldn't let Lindsey's accusation hang there, unchallenged. "You couldn't possibly have seen the driver," she said. "In all this snow? We could barely see the *car!*"

A siren sounded in the distance. A few minutes later, the ambulance slid to a stop in front of the canopy. A minute or two later, a police car arrived. No one was allowed to leave until questions had been asked and, when possible, answered.

It was four o'clock when Hailey and Nell, exhausted and shocked to the core, arrived back in room 416.

"I'm scared, Hailey," Nell said quietly when they had collapsed on their beds. When they'd walked into Devereaux, Michelle, their R.A., had informed them that all classes and extra-curricular activities had been canceled because of the storm. There was no place they had to be. "I *hate* what's happening here."

"I'm scared, too," Hailey admitted. "And I'm frozen to the bone. I don't think I'll ever be warm again." Donning a thick white terrycloth robe over her jeans and sweater, she said, "I didn't like Richard. He was such a creep that night at the Sigma party, agreeing to take Darlene off Robert Q's hands for twenty-five bucks. But I never wished he were *dead*. I still can't believe that he *is*."

Nell began shivering. Pulling the bedspread around her until only her face and hands were uncovered, she leaned against the wall behind the bed. "Hailey, don't get mad, but do you think there's any possibility that . . . well, that Lindsey had a point about Darlene?"

Before Hailey could answer, Nell continued, "Look, you just said it yourself. Darlene had plenty of reason to be furious with Richard. When you told me about the party, you said Darlene *heard* Richard agreeing to take her home. For money. She must have *hated* him for that."

"Well, so did *I*!" Hailey said heatedly, "but it never occurred to me to run him down! And

I'm . . . " The picture of Darlene viciously slashing Robert Q's sweater darted back into her mind. "I'm . . . sure it never crossed Darlene's mind, either." But she was painfully aware that her words lacked conviction.

Nell looked unconvinced.

"I can settle this right now," Hailey announced. "I'm going to call Darlene in Willowcreek. If she's there, she couldn't have been at the mall this afternoon, okay?" She said it forcefully, but secretly she was wondering if Darlene would *be* there. And if she wasn't, where *was* she? Here, in Twin Falls? If she was, why hadn't she called? Maybe she didn't want Hailey to *know* she was back.

Or . . . that she'd never left.

"Willowcreek is only two hours from here," Nell muttered.

"There's a blizzard going on out there, Nell!" Hailey yelled in exasperation. "It took the shuttle forty minutes to make the ten-minute trip from town just now."

Nell sighed and nodded. "You're right. Today is definitely not a good day for a quick road trip. Okay, you call. If Darlene is there, at her grandmother's, I'll agree that she wasn't in that car at the mall. Fair enough?"

Without answering, Hailey picked up the phone to call Darlene. And realized she didn't have the number. She'd scribbled it on a piece of paper when Darlene gave it to her over the phone. Where had she put that piece of paper? If she'd left it lying around in room 242, it was gone forever. Hadn't she put it in her purse? The black shoulder bag?

Hailey's purchases, in snow-dampened plastic bags, were piled on the floor beside her bed. Her purse should have been there, too. But . . . it wasn't.

"What's the matter?" Nell asked.

"I don't have the number. It's in my purse." Hailey fumbled around near the packages. Then she stood up and glanced around the room. "It's not here. My purse isn't here. The black shoulder bag. What did I do with it?"

"Haven't seen it. You didn't hang it in the closet, did you?"

"Why would I do that? Help me look, will you?"

Because the room was still so bare, the search didn't take long. They found no black shoulder bag.

"Where do you remember having it last?" Nell asked. "You must have had it in the drugstore when you paid for your stuff."

"I did. And I had it at the food court. I remember taking my wallet out to pay for the tacos. But . . ." Hailey sat down on the bed.

"Nell, I'm not sure I grabbed my purse off the chair when we left to catch the shuttle."

Nell thought for a minute. Then, "Hailey, I don't remember seeing your purse hanging on your chair. If I had, I would have said something. I would have told you to stash it under the table so no one walking by could snatch it."

Hailey nodded. "Yeah, you would have. You're more paranoid than I am. But . . . if my purse wasn't on the chair, where *was* it? I'm sure I hung it there when I got to the table."

"Well, I went to get fries, remember? But *you* were at the table. Wouldn't you have noticed if someone was trying to take your purse?"

Hailey's face flushed as recollection dawned. "Oh, Nell," she said reluctantly, "I went *back* to the counter. Just for a second. I'd forgotten to grab one of those little packets of salad dressing. So I went back to get it. And I . . . I don't remember taking my purse with me."

"You left your purse hanging in plain sight and went to the counter? While I was getting fries?"

"Well, you don't need to make it sound like I'm too stupid to live! I was only gone a second."

Nell shrugged. "Did you have a lot of money in your purse? Credit cards?"

"No. I spent most of my cash in the drug-store. And my credit card is in the back pocket of my jeans. But . . ." Hailey looked at Nell with troubled eyes. "Nell, my *keys* are in that purse. Including my car keys and my key to this room. If someone stole my purse, they have those keys. The room key has a Deve-reaux tag on it *and* the room number. And after everything that's happened lately . . ." Hailey fell silent, chewing nervously on her lower lip.

Nell huddled deeper within her blanket co-coon as the wind howled outside. The lights flickered ominously. "Maybe your purse wasn't stolen. Maybe you just forgot it and some nice, honest person turned it in at the mall's lost-and-found. You should call and check."

Hailey promptly took Nell's advice. But there was no answer at the mall. The mall must have closed because of the bad weather. Hailey wouldn't find out until tomorrow if her keys were in safe hands or if . . . she couldn't think about the "if." Not now.

The expression on Hailey's face gave her away.

"No answer?" Nell asked.

"No," Hailey said, hanging up the phone. "The mall must be closed."

"Then there's still hope. Listen, Hailey, I've been thinking ever since we got back. Why didn't Richard get out of the way of that car?"

"What?"

"Why didn't he *move*? We were all screaming at him to get out of the way. So why didn't he?"

Hailey went to the window to look out. There was nothing to see but blowing snow and the pale yellow glow of lights in dorms and from the lampposts scattered across campus. "Maybe Richard didn't hear us. The storm was so noisy."

Nell leaned forward on the bed. "But that's just it. It shouldn't have made any difference whether or not he heard us. If you saw a car racing straight toward you, you'd instinctively jump out of the way, right? Anyone would. Unless — "

Hailey turned away from the window. "Unless," she finished for Nell, "you recognized the driver and you were positive it was someone who would never run you down. Then you'd think it was just a joke and you'd think the driver was going to stop at the very last second. Like a game of chicken."

"Right!" Nell said. "That's exactly what I've been thinking. Maybe Richard wasn't waving his arms because he was *mad*. Maybe he was clowning around. Because he knew the person behind the wheel would never actually hit him."

"Someone he knew," Hailey mused aloud. "Someone he was positive wouldn't run him down? A friend?"

"Or a girl," Nell said pointedly. "Richard was a sexist pig. He would never expect a girl to do something so Rambo."

The shrilling of the phone startled both girls.

"Maybe that's Darlene," Hailey said. "I can ask her where she was this afternoon." She glared at Nell. "Even though *I* already know the answer."

But it wasn't Darlene. It was Finn.

"I heard about Wentworth," he said. "Someone told me you were there. It must have been awful."

Hailey leaned against the wall. It was nice to know he'd been thinking about her. "It was horrible. I still can't believe it happened."

"No classes tomorrow. Canceled because of the weather *and*, I guess, because of Richard, too. Everyone is in shock. Someone who saw the whole thing said it was deliberate . . . like murder. No accident, I mean."

"No, it definitely wasn't an accident. But . . ."

"What?"

"Well, Nell and I were just talking about it. Richard could have jumped out of the way. Should have. He had time. And he didn't do it. We think it had to be because he knew the driver and believed the guy was just playing around."

"You think someone Richard *knew* ran him down?"

"It's the only thing that makes sense."

Finn was silent for a moment. Then he said, "Like who?"

Hailey almost said, "According to Nell, like Darlene." But she held back the words. Saying them aloud would give them life, make them too real.

"I don't know," she said instead.

# Chapter 13

Hailey's sleep that night was broken by the nightmarish image of Richard Wentworth's body flying through the air. When she was awakened in the morning by the shrill ringing of the telephone, she felt tense and irritable.

It was shortly after nine o'clock when she answered the phone. Devereaux Hall was quiet. With no classes scheduled, everyone was sleeping in.

"Hailey, it's me, Darlene. I heard about Richard. Robert Q must be devastated! I tried calling Sigma Chi, but they told me he wasn't there. I know they were lying."

And I know who *told* them to lie, Hailey thought. She tugged her robe more tightly around her and pulled the phone out into the hall so she wouldn't wake Nell, even though Nell seemed capable of sleeping through anything. "Are you still in Willowcreek, Darlene?"

"Well, sure, Hailey. I'd have called and told you if I was back in Twin Falls."

So that *hadn't* been Darlene in the drugstore. Unless . . . unless she was lying. "How did you hear about Richard?"

"It was on the news. I couldn't believe it. I called my brother and he filled me in. Poor Gerrie!"

It was the first time Darlene had mentioned Gerrie since the night of the party. "Gerrie?"

"Sure. She and Richard had grown very close. I have a friend who works at the hospital. Mimi said Richard visited Gerrie a lot. Brought her flowers, candy. He even read to her."

*"Richard?"*

"Yeah. Mimi said Robert Q showed up one afternoon and he and Richard had a fight about it. Right there in the hospital."

Hailey remembered Lindsey insisting that she'd recognized the driver of the car. If it was Robert Q she'd recognized, would she have said so? No. Not in a million years. She'd have lied and said it was someone else.

Was Robert Q the jealous type? Possessive? Exactly how angry would he get if a friend of his who had once dated Gerrie began moving in on her again?

"I didn't think Robert Q cared about Gerrie

anymore," Hailey said, "now that Gerrie isn't
. . . perfect anymore."

That comment seemed to delight Darlene. "I
think you're right, Hailey. The fight must have
been about something else."

Realizing her mistake, Hailey quickly
changed the subject. "Darlene, have you heard
from Bo?" The police still hadn't told her what,
if anything, they'd learned about Bo.

"Bo? No. Why would I? He knows we're
through. I told him it was Robert Q I loved,
the night of the Sigma Chi party."

*Before* Gerrie was hit by that rock, Hailey
wondered, or *after*?

"I can't imagine why Gerrie would pick Richard over Robert Q," Darlene said, switching
the subject again. "Richard was a really terrible person. Remember how he wanted money
from Robert Q to take me home from the party?
I don't think I've *ever*," she added heatedly,
"hated anyone as much as I hated Richard that
night. So," she said, her voice abruptly calm
again, "if anyone expects *me* to be shattered
by what happened to Richard, they'll be disappointed."

Darlene had obviously rewritten the party
scene. No one could convince her now that her
version was pure fiction. She blamed Richard,

not Robert Q. And she'd *hated* Richard because of it.

How *much* had she hated Richard? Enough to make the two-hour trip from Willowcreek to Twin Falls in a raging blizzard?

"Poor Robert Q," Darlene said in an odd singsong voice. "First Gerrie ends up in the hospital, probably blind forever, and now Richard is dead. Robert Q must be feeling just awful. Pretty soon, all he'll have left is *me*."

The statement sickened Hailey. Darlene didn't sound at all unhappy about Robert Q having only one "friend" left . . . as long as it was *her*.

Then, briskly, Darlene continued, "Tell Robert Q to *call* me. I can't get through to him at that stupid fraternity house. And I really need to tell him how sorry I am."

Although Hailey dutifully took the phone number again, the phrase "tell him how sorry I am" continued to ring in her ears as she quietly crept back to room 416. Did Darlene mean she was sorry the same way other people were sorry about Richard's death?

Or was there some reason why Darlene should be sorrier than everyone else?

I am so tired, Hailey thought wearily, of all these questions. When is *someone* going to give me some answers?

Nell was still sound asleep, buried beneath her blankets. There would be no morning run today.

Hailey went to the window. She was momentarily stunned to see the snow blanket coming alive with people. Dressed in warm clothing, they were beginning to build snowmen or snow forts. Some were making and hoarding an arsenal of fat, firm snowballs. Others lay down on their backs in the snow and swept their arms and legs in arcs, creating snow angels. Everyone seemed to be having fun.

Hailey's first reaction was shock. They were *playing*! How could they be playing when someone had *died*?

But just as quickly, she realized that while many people on campus had known who Richard was, they wouldn't *all* be mourning his death. And those who hadn't known him had no reason not to enjoy the clear blue sky, bright sunshine, and three feet of fresh, packable snow.

I wouldn't mind forgetting everything that's happened and making a few snow angels myself, Hailey thought as Nell began to stir. We're all sick to death of this awful nightmare. Maybe playing like little kids is what we all need.

So, an hour later when Pete showed up and, a few minutes later, Finn, and asked if Hailey and Nell could "come out and play," Hailey said yes, feeling only a twinge of guilt.

Pete handed her something soft and black and bulky.

"My purse!" Hailey cried with relief. "Where on earth did you find it? I thought it had been stolen."

"When I signed in downstairs and the girl at the desk saw your room number, she asked if I'd bring your purse up. She said it was under her desk when she came on duty this morning. She checked inside for identification and found your room key. Thought I'd save her a trip upstairs."

"That's Pete for you," Finn said, smiling. "We used to call him Fido, because he was always retrieving things. Bringing old shoes home, old newspapers, just like a puppy."

"I didn't know you guys grew up together," Nell said.

Pete laughed. "Who said we grew up? Didn't we just ask you to come out and play?"

Hailey was busy checking the contents of the shoulder bag. "My wallet's still here . . . the money's still in it . . . and . . ." She dangled a key ring triumphantly at Nell . . . "My keys! So there's no weirdo running around out there with a key to our door, Nell."

Finn's brown eyes narrowed. "You thought

someone might have a key to your room? I hope you were planning to call maintenance and have the lock changed."

"Well, we *would* have," she said, flushing slightly because the thought hadn't occurred to her. "Anyway, thanks for bringing my purse. See," she said to Nell, "there *are* honest people out there. I must have left my purse on the shuttle, not at the food court. Someone found it, maybe the driver, and brought it here without removing a single thing." Hailey grinned. "That should give your rampant paranoia a good, swift kick."

"Sometimes," Pete defended Nell, "it *pays* to be paranoid."

Nell sent him a grateful smile.

"Look," Finn said, "why don't we put all this stuff on a back burner and get outside? Fresh air, sunshine, all that snow . . . let's have some fun."

It'll take more than a romp in the snow to make things better, Hailey thought. A *lot* more. But she was as anxious to get outside as everyone else.

And Finn was right. It *did* help. Inside, the dorm was still and somber, library-quiet. But outside, the air rang with shouts and laughter and the whoosh of snowballs speeding from one snow fort to another.

The residents of Nightingale Hall had made the snowy trek to campus to join in the fun. Hailey found a moment alone with Jess to ask if she'd heard anything new about Gerrie. "Has she gone to Philadelphia yet for her surgery?"

Jess shook her head. "Not yet. The weather's been too bad. Cath Devon told me that Gerrie heard about Richard's death on the *news*! Can you believe it?" She glanced balefully toward a large snow fort off to her left. "Robert Q didn't even have the decency to go to the hospital and break the news himself to Gerrie. I know she and Richard were friends. It was cruel to let her find out that way."

The fort, whose snowy walls should have melted under Jess's angry glare was manned by Robert Q, Lyle, Puffy, and Susan, all wearing expensive pastel-colored skiwear.

"To look at the four of them," Hailey said contemptuously, "you'd never guess that a close friend of theirs was killed yesterday."

"I heard Robert Q tell someone that 'good old Richard' wouldn't have wanted them to mope around," Jess said.

Hailey made a face of distaste. "That's what people always say to hide the fact that they have less compassion than a pencil-point. I'm sure Richard would not have been happy to see Robert Q and his fan club frolicking in the snow the day after he was killed."

"Could we please just ignore them?" Nell said, bending to fill her gloved hands with snow. "We're supposed to be having *fun!*"

And, in spite of everything, they *did* have fun. Hailey let herself feel safe, outside on the Commons surrounded by friends, and lost herself in the moment.

But when the sun disappeared behind a thick bank of clouds, wet fingers and feet began to feel the cold. People began drifting away.

"I'm freezing," Nell said. Her cheeks were wind-chafed, the tip of her nose bright red. "Let's go in."

And Hailey reluctantly returned to reality. Nothing had changed. Back in 416, Hailey changed her clothes and, a while later, left for the library. "I've goofed off all day," she told Nell. "Time to get back to work." What she really wanted was some time alone, to think, and the library was the best place to do that. "See you later."

Darkness was falling quickly, and as she hurried across campus, she found herself looking over her shoulder repeatedly. Maybe trekking across campus alone wasn't such a hot idea. Maybe she should have talked Nell into coming with her.

No! she told herself, huddling deeper within

her jacket. I can take care of myself.

But she hurried her steps. And breathed a sigh of relief when she reached the wide stone steps of the library.

When she left an hour later, she decided to go to Butler Hall, the administration building, to see what she could find out about Darlene's brother. Mike . . . wasn't that his name? She could at least find out if he lived on or off campus. Maybe he could answer some of her questions about both Darlene *and* Bo.

She hurried across the Commons toward the big, brick building. Darlene's brother should be able to tell her if Darlene really *had* been in Willowcreek all this time.

But the only office open in the administration building was the Dean's office. Hailey would have hurried past it if she hadn't heard Susan Grossbeck's voice shouting, "This is ridiculous! You're accusing me of *cheating*?"

Alone in the dimly lit hall, Hailey stopped in her tracks.

Puffy's unmistakable whine quickly followed Susan's voice. "Dr. Leonardo knows Susan and I study together. That's why our test papers were so similar. But we *didn't* cheat!"

Hailey moved closer to the glass-windowed door. Dr. Leonardo was a history professor. Hailey wasn't taking history, but Susan *was* in her math class, and she was the smartest student in there. Why would Susan need to cheat on a test?

The Dean murmured something Hailey didn't catch.

Then Susan said airily, "Besides, everyone knows two great minds think as one, right?"

"Well, that wouldn't apply in *this* case, would it?" Dr. Leonardo shot back sarcastically. "On the basis of this remarkable coincidence, combined with an anonymous telephone call I received this morning, I requested and received permission to open your tennis locker."

"My locker?" Susan sounded appalled. "You got a mysterious phone call telling you to search my locker? For what?"

"In your locker, Ms. Grossbeck," Dr. Leonardo answered, coldly, "a security officer found my personal notes for the test in question, which you could only have obtained from my desk drawer. It was very generous of you to share those notes with Ms. Wycroft. Unfortunately, she may question your generosity when Dr. Lambert dispenses her disciplinary action. I, on the other hand," she added with a slight smile, "shall be looking forward to that moment."

Hailey had heard enough. She turned and hurried from the building.

# Chapter 14

Finn and Pete were in room 416 when Hailey returned. When she had related the conversation she'd overheard, Nell said with delight, "Well, well, well! I knew Susan and Puffy were disgusting little snobs, but I didn't know they were cheats!"

"I'm not so sure they are," Hailey said.

"You're defending *Susan?*" Nell asked, disbelief in her voice.

"Susan is in my calculus class," Hailey answered. "She's the smartest person in there. She doesn't need to cheat."

"Maybe," Pete said, "she just stole the notes to prove that she could *do* it. An ego thing. Probably thought she'd never get caught."

"I heard Dr. Leonardo say that she'd received an anonymous phone call," Hailey said as she took a seat on the floor beside Finn. "Telling her to look in Susan's tennis locker. Don't you think that's pretty weird? If Susan *had* stolen those notes, she wouldn't *tell* anyone. Except Puffy, of course. And Puffy would never turn Susan in. So who made that phone call?"

"Who knows?" Nell asked. "Who cares?"

"Well," Hailey pressed, "either Susan *didn't* cheat and someone is framing her, or Susan *did* steal the notes and then made the mistake of telling someone she shouldn't have trusted. I don't think she'd be that stupid." Although, Hailey quickly reminded herself, Richard Wentworth had been that stupid. He'd trusted someone not to hit him. He'd been wrong. And now he was . . . dead.

Hailey felt depression settling in her bones. "This doesn't make any sense. I thought whoever wrecked our room was mad at us for helping Darlene. But Susan and Puffy didn't help Darlene. Just the opposite. So, if they're being framed, it can't be by the same person who's mad at *us*."

"Probably doesn't have anything to do with what happened in your room," Finn said. "And you can't even be sure they *are* being framed. Do you really think those two are above cheating?"

Hailey shook her head. "I don't know. Maybe not." But she couldn't shake the feeling of uneasiness created by the overheard conver-

sation in the Dean's office. It made no sense
. . . but then, what *did* these days?

Pete and Nell had already tuned out Hailey's
questions and were huddled together on a corner of Nell's bed, talking quietly. Noticing,
Hailey's spirits lifted. Pete and Nell? That
might be nice, since Pete and Finn were
friends. And she hadn't heard that Pete was
dating anyone else.

If only all she had to think about was ro-
mance . . .

Hailey saw Susan only once the next day.
And when they passed in the library, she saw
far more pain than anger in Susan's eyes. Being
caught cheating at Salem was a very big deal.
Hailey had no trouble imagining what kind of
day Susan was having: the stares, the gossip,
the contemptuous attitude of her professors.

At noon, Hailey heard that Susan and Puffy
had been suspended from the tennis team until
their disciplinary hearing, which was scheduled
for a week away.

A week! And Susan and Puffy were going
through this alone, since Robert Q, Lyle, and
their other "friends" were avoiding them as if
they'd come down with a contagious disease.

That evening when Hailey, Nell, Pete, and
Finn went to Vinnie's for pizza, Robert Q and

Lyle were in one booth, both with dates, while Susan and Puffy sat alone in a corner booth.

"It must be horrible, being gossiped about all over campus," Hailey said. She felt almost certain that the two had been framed. Whoever had wreaked revenge on Robert Q and Richard had struck again.

But she had no proof.

"Don't waste your sympathy on those two," Nell cautioned. "Save it for someone like *us*. At least their *room* wasn't wrecked."

"Or Darlene," Finn said. "She probably got hurt worse than anyone."

Hailey look at him, surprised. As he left to have their soda pitcher refilled, she watched him with a feeling of warmth. It was nice that he cared when someone got hurt.

When Finn returned with a full pitcher, he had four friends from Nightingale Hall with him. They were deep into a conversation about Richard's car, which had been found by the state police. There were no fingerprints in or on the car. And the blowing snow had erased any telltale footprints left when Richard's killer abandoned the "murder weapon" and hiked away.

But the biggest clue, to Hailey, was the car's location. It was halfway between Twin Falls and Willowcreek.

There were just too many unanswered questions about Darlene. When Hailey returned to the dorm, the first thing she did was call Darlene at her grandmother's.

The conversation was as disturbing as the last time Hailey had talked with Darlene.

Darlene refused to talk about Gerrie or Richard. She wanted to talk about Puffy and Susan. "They'll be leaving campus now, won't they, Hailey? Won't they be kicked out? Sent home?"

"I don't know, Darlene. They haven't had their hearing yet. No one even knows for sure that they cheated. I don't know why, but I just feel like they were set up."

"What?" Darlene shrieked into the phone. "Hailey, you're not on *their* side now, are you?"

Hailey sighed. "I'm not on anybody's *side*, Darlene. This isn't a *war*." Oh, isn't it? a little voice in her head teased.

"They *have* to be sent home," Darlene said in a low, grating voice. Then, her tone becoming mournful, she added, "Poor Robert Q. He just isn't going to have anyone left on campus, *is* he? I *wish* I could be there for him now. My parents are back in Twin Falls, but I can't come back yet. Soon, though."

Then she began talking nonstop, in a high, breathless voice, only of Robert Q: how lonely he must be, how much he must need her, how hard it was to be away from him when she wanted desperately to be there, comforting him.

Hailey felt as if she'd wandered into one of Darlene's dreams. Not once since Darlene left Twin Falls had Robert Q asked about her. He hadn't asked Hailey for a phone number where Darlene could be reached. He hadn't driven over to see her, a trip which, with his yellow Miata and without speed traps or state troopers, wouldn't take much more than ninety minutes. Maybe seventy-five.

Robert Q Parker had not shown the slightest bit of interest in the town girl named Darlene Riggs after she'd left Twin Falls.

Yet here was Darlene, yearning to be with Robert Q to *comfort* him.

It was so unreal.

Either Darlene has fallen through the looking glass, Hailey thought, or *I* have.

What had happened to Darlene's grip on reality? And how *much* of it had she lost?

While Nell curled up in bed with a textbook, Hailey paced the worn blue carpet. She needed to talk to someone about Darlene. But who? She didn't know Darlene's parents well enough. Besides, they had enough on their minds, with Darlene's grandmother ill.

Darlene's brother, Mike. He was on campus somewhere. He must know about Robert Q and everything else that had happened. And he certainly should know Darlene better than anyone else on campus.

Where could she find Mike Riggs?

She'd ask around tomorrow.

The next day, the snow that had looked so beautiful when it first blanketed campus, was rapidly turning into a sea of gray slush. The temperature had warmed only a few degrees, but that was enough to begin the melting while the sun shone brightly.

There seemed to be police officers everywhere, asking questions. If only, Hailey thought, they had the *answers*. What had happened to that suspect the one officer had told her about? Why hadn't he been arrested? Or . . . she.

Hailey asked several people about Mike Riggs. No one seemed to have heard of him. It was eerie, as if Darlene's brother didn't really exist.

Finally, Hailey decided to call Darlene's house. If Mike Riggs wasn't there, his mother would know where to reach him. That would be the first thing she'd do when she got back to the dorm.

But . . . it wasn't.

When she unlocked the door to 416 and pulled it open, she was greeted by a blast of air so cold, it took her breath away.

The wide window on the opposite side of the room had been cranked outward as far as it would go. There was no screen in place.

The room was every bit as cold as the outside.

"I don't *believe* this!" Hailey gasped, tossing her books on her bed. "Nell left the window wide open? Is she *nuts*?"

She rushed across the room to crank the window closed.

She was reaching down for the curving brass handle set into the windowsill when she realized, too late, that Nell would never have left a window wide open on a day when the temperature was barely above freezing.

Someone *else* had opened the window.

And then she heard a soft, whispering rush behind her, and a sharp, forceful blow struck her left side, knocking her off-balance.

"Gotcha!" a voice hissed, and a second shove toppled Hailey off her feet.

She pitched forward out of the fourth-floor window.

# Chapter 15

The terrifying moment when jagged, half-frozen mounds of dirty snow rushed up to meet Hailey seemed to last an eternity.

Too breathless to scream, she closed her eyes.

But they flew open again as her body was suddenly, cruelly, yanked to a standstill.

And then she was hanging from the window, spinning crazily from the force of her abrupt stop. Something was tugging painfully at her chest and shoulder. Terrified and dazed, she was vaguely conscious of movement above her, at the window, and of someone cursing.

She stopped spinning, and hung at a slight angle. What was holding her up? It hurt, pulling so harshly at her chest and shoulder . . . but if it gave way, if it broke . . .

Dizziness overwhelmed her. She could feel the icy ground far beneath her . . . waiting for whatever was holding her up to break and send her plunging to the ice below.

People hurrying across campus saw her and gathered below her, staring up in disbelief at the figure hanging precariously from a fourth-floor window of Devereaux Hall.

Lost in shock and terror, Hailey thought she heard a door slam above her . . . was he gone? Or was he still there at the window, trying to remove whatever it was that was keeping her from plummeting to the icy ground below?

Her chest hurt. Her shoulder was on fire. The gentle swaying motion was making her sick.

She wanted to scream, but she couldn't. Terror had stolen her voice.

Everything after that was a blur.

There were more shouts. There were voices, calling up to her. There were doors slamming, windows cranking open, more shouting.

The nauseating swaying motion stopped. And her mind stopped, too. Because the realization that whatever was holding her up, away from the cold, hard ground could, at any second, break or *be* broken and allow her to fall, was unbearable. She stopped thinking, stopped feeling. She closed her eyes and mind. She didn't even feel the cold.

What brought her back to awareness was

Finn's voice above her warning, "Easy, easy, pull *slowly*!" And Pete's voice said, "Watch her arm there," and Nell, her voice shaking with fear, asked, "Is she conscious? *Is* she?"

And Hailey was being pulled upward, very slowly. After what seemed like hours, she felt herself being pulled over the sill and into her room. They had been very careful with her. And then she was on her bed, shaken and dazed and dizzy, but *alive*.

Hailey opened her eyes.

She hadn't fallen.

She hadn't died.

She was *alive*.

Something soft and bulky was being slipped up, away from her chest, and over her head.

"Are you okay?" Finn asked.

She looked up at him. "No. I'm not. But I will be."

He was holding up her purse, the black shoulder bag with the extra-long strap.

"This," Finn said, "is what saved your life."

Hailey stared at him blankly. "My purse?"

"Yep. The strap caught on the window crank. Acted like a sling holding you up."

"Actually," Nell said, her voice a bit shaky, "you can thank *me*, Hailey. Remember, I told you to wear the strap across your chest, so no one could run by and snatch your purse off your shoulder?" She smiled weakly. "This time, my paranoia came in handy, didn't it?"

"It sure did," Pete agreed. To Hailey, he said, "The strap made a kind of harness for you when you fell."

"You were *very* lucky," Finn said.

"But I didn't *fall*." Hailey began to tremble from shock, cold, and fear.

The three stared at her.

"I didn't fall," she repeated. "I was pushed." Remembering accelerated her trembling. Her teeth began to chatter.

Finn turned quickly to crank the window shut and lock it. Nell grabbed a blanket from her bed to wrap, shawl-like, around Hailey's shoulders.

"Someone pushed you?" Pete asked. "Are you sure?"

Hailey nodded. "When I came home, the window was wide open. I ran over to close it and . . . and something hit me. *Someone*. And when I didn't fall right away, he hit me again. And I went out the window. If my purse strap hadn't got caught on that crank . . ." She closed her eyes, shuddering.

Finn moved to the bed to place a comforting arm around her shoulders.

"Hailey," Nell said, "we're four stories up. You . . . you could have been *killed*." Nell's lower lip trembled. "Hailey," she whispered, "this is scary."

"Did you *see* anything?" Finn wanted to know. "Hear anything?"

Hailey thought for a minute. "I heard something . . . soft . . . sneakers, maybe. And after I'd fallen out, I heard him swearing."

"He must have heard us coming," Nell said, "and taken off."

"Did *you* see anyone?" Hailey asked. Her trembling had finally stopped, but her face was gray. "Out in the hall?"

"No. Not a soul."

When campus security and then the town police asked Hailey later if she had any idea who her attacker might have been, she stared at them from her bed and said, "I don't know." She thought about Darlene's rage the night of the pizza party, and Robert Q's fury when his car burned, and Bo Jessup's anger the night of the Sigma Chi party. "Did you check out Bo Jessup like I asked you to?"

"Couldn't have been him," an officer said cryptically. "Left town. His mother says he left without a word."

"Well, where *is* he?" Hailey's eyes swept the room, as if she expected to find Bo Jessup lurking in a corner.

"Don't know yet, Miss. But we'll find him."

"When?" Hailey demanded. "*When* did Bo leave town?"

"Not sure, Miss. No one seems to know. When we locate him, we'll let you know."

"Was he the suspect one of the officers told me about?"

"Can't say, Miss." Armed with Hailey's statement, the officers left.

Hailey sank down among her blankets. So many questions were spinning around in her brain, just as she had been spinning, so high above the ground, a short while ago.

If Pete hadn't brought her purse back . . . if she hadn't worn it the way Nell told her to . . .

Shuddering, Hailey burrowed deeper within her blankets.

*Where* was Bo Jessup? And *how* angry *was* he?

# Chapter 16

Hailey stayed in bed all the next day, too shaken to leave her room. Nell, Amy, and Jess took turns staying with her so she wouldn't be alone.

But by the following day, she was too restless to stay inside, and went to class, in spite of the constant, painful throb in her right shoulder.

Everyone she encountered on campus wanted to talk about what one girl called Hailey's "near-death experience."

Hailey couldn't stand it. That was the very last thing she wanted to talk about. How could people be so insensitive? Couldn't they see that talking about it brought back a flood of terror? Couldn't they see the fear in her eyes, see her hands begin to shake? She kept seeing the snow-covered ground rising up to meet her . . .

At noon, she took refuge in the administration building, where she began a search for Darlene's brother Mike. Darlene had said she and Bo dated in high school. So wouldn't Mike Riggs know something about Bo? He might even know where Bo would have gone when he left town.

There was no Mike Riggs listed in the university's records.

She sought out a clerk, a harried-looking woman carrying an armload of papers. "Are students who commute listed separately from resident students?" Hailey asked.

"If they're part-time," the woman answered. "Only a class or two, that kind of thing. Wouldn't be in the directory. Ask over there." She pointed to a young man in a dark suit sitting at a desk. "George can help you out."

But George was no help at all. After flipping through a pile of folders neatly stacked on his desk, he shook his head. "I've got all the part-timers right here," he said, patting the pile of folders. "No Michael Riggs."

"But I know he's a student here," Hailey protested. "Are you *sure* he's not in there?"

The young man looked insulted. "If he was a part-timer," he said haughtily, "he'd be *in* here. And he's *not*." And he swiveled his chair around so that his back was to Hailey.

It was clear that she'd been dismissed.

She left Butler Hall despondent. The only other person she could ask about Bo was Darlene, and all *she* wanted to talk about was Robert Q. Besides, Hailey still had plenty of questions about Darlene.

Hailey had to find Mike Riggs.

Why not try their house, she thought suddenly. Even if Darlene's brother isn't there, one of his parents might be. They can tell me where to find Mike.

If they wanted to know why she was looking for him, she'd make up something. No point in worrying them about Darlene.

She didn't want to go alone. She didn't want to go *anywhere* alone. Someone had tried to kill her, and no one knew who that someone was.

She didn't even know what or who to watch out for.

Which meant she might tell the *wrong* person that she was going to Darlene's.

Better to go alone.

So, in spite of a queasy stomach, after classes Hailey went straight to the blue Ford and drove downtown.

When she passed the diner, she wondered if Finn was working.

When she passed the mall, its parking lot half-filled with cars bearing university stickers, she wondered if he was in there.

Stop thinking about Finn Conran, she scolded mentally. You don't have time for romantic feelings now. Not with everything else that's happening.

And then when she pulled up in front of the tired gray house on Fourth Street, there was Finn, making his way down the icy steps.

If he was surprised to see her at Darlene's, he didn't show it. He smiled and said, "Hi. How are you feeling?" when she joined him at the foot of the steps.

"I'm fine." Hailey glanced up at the house. "Darlene hasn't come home, has she?"

Finn shook his head. "Nope. Still in Willowcreek."

Hailey decided he looked very good, standing there, the collar of his brown jacket turned up against the wind, his prominent cheekbones red with cold. His hair could use a comb, but then, her own hair had lost its battle with the wind the minute she stepped out of the dorm that morning.

"Your hair looks great," Finn said.

Hailey laughed. Then she remembered why she was there. "Is anybody home?" she asked.

"Nope. I was looking for Darlene, too. I thought she might have a clue about who pushed you out that window. She might know where Jessup is, too. But she's not here. Nobody's home."

Hailey swallowed her disappointment. If Mike Riggs wasn't home, she wasn't going to get any answers today. Her questions would have to wait.

"How did you get here?" she asked Finn.

"I hitched." He grinned down at her. "If you're headed back to campus, feel like giving a foot soldier a ride?"

And then Hailey allowed herself, just for a little while, to put all of the horror behind her and focus only on the moment at hand. "It'll cost you. A burger, maybe? At the diner?"

"Done," Finn said cheerfully. "But that's not much of a fare for a ride back to school. I get a discount at the diner, remember?"

"Well, maybe I'll think of something else," Hailey teased, surprising herself, and then quickly added, "fries, maybe."

They got into the car laughing, but Hailey hadn't even hit the first stop sign when Finn said, "We need to talk about yesterday. I think you were targeted because of Darlene. That's been the connection in every incident. Gerrie, Robert Q, Richard — they all knew Darlene. And if you're right that Susan and Puffy were set up, well, they knew her, too. That bothers me."

Hailey felt a rush of warmth. It bothered Finn that she wasn't safe: He worried about her? Didn't that mean he cared?

That would be nice. Very nice.

She felt a little less alone.

"But I wasn't rotten to Darlene," she said. "At least, I don't think I was."

"No, you weren't. But maybe our crazy doesn't *know* that, or doesn't *care*. Maybe he's out to get everyone on this campus who even *knew* Darlene."

Hailey shuddered. Where, she wondered, was Bo Jessup? Why hadn't the police *found* him? Was he hiding? Did he have reason to hide?

At the diner, they were promptly joined by Jess and Ian. Neither of them noticed Hailey's lack of enthusiasm. She had been looking forward to being alone with Finn. There was still so much she didn't know about him.

Telling herself she should be grateful for their concern, Hailey slid over in the booth to make room for Jess.

"Hailey," Jess asked after they had all ordered, "how did someone get into your room? Did you forget to lock the door?" She didn't add the word "again," but Hailey heard it, anyway.

Irritated, she said, "No. It was locked. And the police said there was no sign of forced entry."

"Then doesn't that mean someone had a key?" Ian asked. "Who, besides you and Nell, had a key?"

"I guess the security guards have a passkey. But why would anyone *else* have a key?"

The diner had become so crowded, they had to lean over the table, heads together, to hear each other.

"You didn't give a key to *anyone*?" Finn asked Hailey.

She shook her head. "Of course not."

"Then someone *stole* a key," Jess suggested.

"No," Hailey said. "Nell and I both have our keys. I *thought* someone had my keys. My purse was missing. I thought it had been stolen at the mall. But I'd just left it on the shuttle. Someone brought it to the dorm, and my keys were still in it."

"How long was your purse missing?" Ian asked.

"It was brought to the dorm the next morning. Why?"

Ian looked grim. "Because maybe your purse *was* stolen. On purpose. I mean, by someone who knew it was yours, and had seen you put your keys in there. It's really easy to get copies made of keys, Hailey. That way, they wouldn't have to break in."

Hailey had already known someone was out to get her. But the thought that someone had carried out such an elaborate plan — stealing her purse, having her keys copied, and lying in wait in her own room to attack her — made Hailey's skin crawl.

Who hated her that much?

And now that his plan had failed . . . did he have other plans for her?

# Chapter 17

By the time Hailey drove Finn to Lester Dorm, the sun was fading fast. She had always loved the way the tall lamplights stationed around campus cast shadows across the snow and the ivy-covered stone buildings, but now it seemed depressing, even frightening. It was too dark . . .

She pulled the Ford to a stop in front of Lester.

But Finn didn't get out. He turned to face her on the front seat. "Hailey," he said, "I don't want to worry you, but if someone made a copy of your room key, he must still have it. You and Nell should have your lock changed. Better yet, ask for a different room."

"No!" she said firmly. "We've already moved once. We're not doing it again. We'll put a chair under the doorknob and tomorrow we'll see about changing the locks. But that creep is not chasing us out of our room. Not this time."

Finn grinned. "Now, how did I know you'd say that? Though it was worth a try. Chair under the doorknob sounds good." He looked at her for a moment with the same expression he'd had on his face after they pulled her back to safety. Then he leaned forward, put an arm around her shoulders to pull her close to him, and kissed her. He smelled of winter, crisp and clean, but there was nothing cold about his kiss.

It lasted a long time.

And for those lovely, long seconds, all of the tension and fear left Hailey and she felt only the warmth and caring in Finn's arms around her.

When he lifted his head, he began, "Hailey, I — " Then he stopped, shook his head and said, "Later. Sleep well."

And then he was out of the car. He stood on the curb, watching as she pulled away. In her rearview mirror, she saw him. And thought, he'll be around tomorrow and the next day and the next . . .

She hadn't learned that much about Finn. But she knew now that his best friends were Ian Banion and Pete Torrance, that he was interested in politics and hoped to practice law, and that he had a sense of humor, something Hailey considered essential.

And he had the greatest smile on campus.

She slept fitfully all night, in spite of the straight-backed wooden chair propped under the doorknob. When she awoke in the morning and saw it there, her stomach turned over. I hate it, she thought despairingly, that the bad things disappear during the night while you're asleep but return in the morning when you wake up.

Nell's mood wasn't any better. "You know," she grumbled, rubbing her eyes, "you'd think with all the police hanging around campus all the time, they'd have caught the creep who pushed you out the window. I didn't come to college to sleep with a chair against my door. My parents would have a fit if they knew. Paranoia is hereditary, Hailey. I got it from *them*. They'd yank me out of this school so fast . . ."

Hailey had explained Ian's theory about the key to Nell the night before. "Look, Nell," she said now as she dressed in jeans and a bulky peach sweater, "all of this has something to do with Darlene. I'm going to try to track down her brother. Mike Riggs. She said he's a student here. Maybe he'll know something."

Nell looked at Hailey uneasily. "Are you going alone?"

Hailey swept her hair up and fastened it with

a clip on top of her head. "I was planning on it. Why?"

"How do you know he's not the one who pushed you?"

Hailey turned around. "Darlene's brother?"

"Yes. Her brother." Nell glanced in the dresser mirror as she stood up, and groaned at her reflection. "Aren't motive and opportunity the two things the cops look for? Well, I'd think Darlene's brother would be really mad about the way everyone, especially Robert Q, treated his sister. That's motive. And since he's a student here, that's opportunity. Right?"

Hailey bent to tie the laces on her boots. "Robert Q had motive and opportunity, too, Nell. And Bo had a motive . . . we just don't know yet if he had the opportunity."

"True. But if Darlene didn't clue her brother in on who were the bad guys and who were the good guys, he could be madder than both Robert Q *and* Bo. What do you know about Darlene's brother?"

"Mike. His name is Mike. And I don't know anything except that he got a scholarship to school. So I guess he's not stupid."

"Do Finn or Pete know him?"

Hailey slapped a navy blue knit cap on her wavy hair. "I don't know. The subject never came up. I'll ask, though. In fact, I think I'll leave a few minutes early and stop by Lester to ask Finn. If he's not already in class. Catch you later."

At Lester Dorm, alive with the frantic sounds of late-risers rushing to get to class, Hailey went directly to the reception desk in the lobby.

A plaid-shirted boy wearing glasses was manning the desk. He looked like he was asleep. He was leaning back in his chair, hands folded over his lap, eyes closed.

"Excuse me," Hailey said. "I'd like to see Finn Conran, please. I don't know what room he's in."

Without moving, the boy said, "He's not in *any* room. No Conran here."

"You didn't even *check*," she protested.

"No need. I know the last name of everyone in this place." Eyes still closed, he tapped his temple with a forefinger. "Photographic memory. Names, room numbers, it's all up here. No one named Conran lives in Lester."

Pompous jerk! "Look," Hailey argued, "I'm sure he lives here. Will you please just *check*?"

"You probably got the name wrong," Pompous Jerk replied lazily. "Next time, double-check before the guy tells you good night."

Hailey had had it. "Only an idiot would get

a name like Finn Conran wrong!" she shrieked.

His lack of reaction told Hailey he thought she qualified.

Giving up, she turned in disgust and stomped from the building.

On her way across the Commons to her ten o'clock class, she ran into Pete. He was dressed in gray sweats and breathing hard, so she knew he'd been jogging or running. It was nice that he and Nell had that in common.

"Listen," Hailey asked abruptly, while Pete jogged in place, "doesn't Finn live at Lester?"

Pete bent to retie his sneaker. "Sure. Why?"

Hailey explained about the encounter in Lester's lobby.

Pete shrugged. "The guy's a jerk. Probably doesn't know what he's talking about."

"Thanks," Hailey said. "Gotta run to my ten o'clock. See ya."

An hour later, as she was coming out of class with Beth Darnell, she remembered that Beth lived at Lester. On an impulse, she asked if Beth had seen Finn that day.

"Um . . . no I haven't. I don't run into him that often. We only have one class together."

Hailey felt her cheeks grow warm. She felt weird talking to someone about Finn. "But you see him every day at Lester, right?"

Beth frowned. "Gee, I don't think Finn lives

at Lester, Hailey. I've never seen him in the building. I figured he lived in a frat house."

Confused again, Hailey thanked her and hurried away.

Beth had seemed every bit as certain that Finn *didn't* live at Lester as Pete had that Finn *did*. If Finn didn't live at Lester, why had he let her think he did? True, he hadn't actually *said* that's where he lived. But that's where he'd asked to be dropped off. Or . . . had she just assumed that's where he lived, and dropped him off there without asking? She couldn't remember.

But if Finn didn't live at Lester . . . where *did* he live?

# Chapter 18

Finn called later that day to invite Hailey and Nell to join him and Pete at Duffy's, a favorite restaurant-bar. Hailey accepted without hesitation, promising to check with Nell and get back to him.

She'd find out tonight where he lived.

Nell couldn't go. "I have a philosophy paper due tomorrow morning. Can't afford to turn it in late. Tell Pete I'm sorry."

But since she wasn't going, Pete decided to stay home and study.

"I guess it's just you and me, kid," Finn said when she called him back. "Pick me up in front of Lester at six?"

He wouldn't have asked her to pick him up there if that wasn't where he lived, Hailey realized. It made sense that Pete, who knew Finn better than Beth did, would know where Finn lived. That idiot at Lester's reception desk must have the brains of a turnip. She'd feel like a total fool asking Finn where he lived when he had clearly told her to pick him up at Lester. She wouldn't even ask.

Duffy's wasn't crowded. The waiter who served Finn and Hailey told them glumly, "Business has been lousy ever since that guy got splattered all over the mall parking lot."

Hailey winced.

The waiter glanced around the normally raucous bar. No one was playing pool. The video games were silent, the photo booths empty. Even the jukebox music seemed subdued. And Hailey noticed that most of the patrons were townspeople, not students. "It's like everyone's afraid the guy who hit and ran is hangin' around in our parking lot," the waiter added, "waitin' to cream another victim."

He *could* be, Hailey thought, her eyes scanning the place from wall to wall. He could be anywhere. And he could be . . . *anyone*.

Before Hailey and Finn had a chance to talk, Milo Keith and Ian Banion arrived from Nightingale Hall and, without waiting for an invitation, sat down at Hailey and Finn's table.

Hailey had no intention of letting that happen again. She was about to hint sharply that four was definitely a crowd, when Ian began talking about the grim situation on campus.

"We all heard what happened to you," Ian told her. "You were really lucky. So, do you think it's over now? Think the guy's given up and crawled back into his hole?"

The feeling of hanging high above the ground, helpless, came over Hailey again. She bit down hard on her lower lip to make the feeling go away. "Why would he hide?" she said irritably. "No one knows who he is. No one seems to have a clue."

Ian leaned forward and explained. "But Jess said you thought the reason for all of this stuff was Darlene, right? That someone wanted revenge for the way she'd been treated?"

Hailey nodded.

"Well," Ian said, "hasn't our resident weirdo finished his self-appointed task? He's done a number on Robert Q, on Gerrie, Richard, maybe even Susan and Puffy. And Lindsey Kite is miserable, too, because her two best friends are in disgrace. Isn't that everyone who made Darlene's life miserable? What we can't figure out is why *you* were targeted. You and Nell didn't stomp on Darlene."

"I'm not sure why, either," Hailey admitted. "Nell and I thought maybe it had something to do with helping Darlene change the way she looked. To please Robert Q. At first, we thought it was Darlene's ex-boyfriend, but the police say Bo wasn't around when all this stuff happened. They don't know *where* he is."

"Well, my point was, isn't that everyone? I mean, if there's a list of people at Salem who gave Darlene a hard time or encouraged her to go after Robert Q, there probably isn't anyone left on that list, is there? So maybe the guy will crawl back into his hole now."

"He has to be *found*!" Hailey cried. "He can't just disappear. He *killed* Richard! And he almost killed *me*!"

"Take it easy," Finn said, laying a hand on Hailey's arm. "At least you and Nell are safe."

Suddenly Hailey sat up very straight, her eyes wide with new fear. "Nell!" she cried, surprising her companions.

"What about her? Ian asked.

"If there *is* a list, Nell might be on it, too. And we . . . I . . . left Nell alone in our room. I never thought — "

"Take it easy," Milo cautioned. "She's in the dorm, right? In your room? The door locks, doesn't it? And there are cops all over the place. She probably couldn't be any safer."

Hailey and Finn exchanged a glance. Hailey said anxiously, "But this person — whoever it is — might have made a copy of my key. He could have a key to our room right this minute!"

Finn threw some money on the table. He

and Hailey ran from the bar without asking Milo or Ian to join them.

Hailey paid little attention to the speed limit signs en route to campus. When the Ford screeched to a halt in front of Devereaux, she and Finn jumped out and ran inside.

They took the stairs two at a time, ignoring the elevator, which was too slow.

When they reached room 416, Hailey still hadn't unearthed the key she'd been fumbling for in her black shoulder bag.

"Pound!" she urged Finn, while she continued to search. "Pound on the door!" She began shouting Nell's name.

Finn rapped sharply, then more loudly. Other doors in the corridor opened, heads peered out tentatively, but the door to 416 remained closed.

"Oh, God," Hailey breathed, her frantic fingers searching, searching, "where *is* she? Why doesn't she answer the door? I never should have left her alone!"

"Nell! Nell!" Hailey shouted, and finally, finally found her key. But her hands were trembling. She thrust the key toward Finn.

Other Devereaux-dwellers, anxious about the shouts and pounding, came from their rooms and moved down the hall toward 416 to see what was going on. They moved slowly, tentatively, clearly afraid of another disaster, another injury, perhaps even another . . . death?

Music drifted from their open doors. They shouldn't be playing music *now*, Hailey thought angrily, not now when Nell might be in trouble . . .

Finn was having trouble with the lock. Just as Hailey was sure she was going to scream in frustration, she heard a click and the door opened.

The room was dark. Hailey sucked in her breath. Nell should have been sitting at her desk, the lamp on, finishing her philosophy paper. But she wasn't.

And the room was silent. Nell never wrote in silence. She said music helped her "creative juices."

Finn flipped the switch beside the door.

When Hailey's eyes found Nell, her heart stopped. Nell was lying face-down on her bed, a pillow completely covering her head.

She's been suffocated, was Hailey's first sickening thought.

At the same moment, her eyes were drawn to a small, round red light glowing on Nell's stereo, situated on a table at the foot of her bed. That tiny light meant Nell's CD player was *on*.

Then, why was it silent instead of blaring like usual? Had Nell's attacker turned it down so no one would come knocking on the door to complain about the noise and discover Nell lying there, unconscious . . . or worse?

Hailey sagged against the doorframe, where a small group of curious onlookers had gathered. "Lift the pillow," she whispered to Finn. "*Lift* it!"

Finn removed the pillow.

They all saw the headphones at the same moment. A unanimous sigh of relief escaped the crowd.

And Nell slept on, headphones on her ears.

Nell was safe.

Hailey went weak with relief. She reached out to gently dislodge the earphones. Nell rolled over, but didn't awaken. Hailey put the earphones on top of the stereo and turned it off. Then she pulled Nell's blankets up around her shoulders, carefully tucking in the edges. "It's going to be really cold tonight," she said in an eerily quiet voice to Finn, who watched her with concern in his eyes. "Can't have my roomie catching pneumonia."

"Everything okay here?" someone in the group in the doorway asked. Hailey, fighting tears of relief, could only nod silently.

"Okay, show's over!" the voice continued.

"Everybody back to their rooms."

Murmuring among themselves, the group turned and left.

Hailey's legs gave out then, and she sank down on her own bed.

Finn sat beside her, his arms around her, until she stopped shaking.

"Are you sure you're okay?" he asked at least twice before he left.

"No, I'm not," she said. "But I'll *be* okay. You go ahead. I'm just going to sit here until my heart quits hammering."

"I'll call you later," he promised after kissing her good night.

"I could call *you*," she offered. "That way, the phone won't ring in here and wake Nell up. What's your room number?"

He shook his head. "I've got to make a quick trip to the library. Research. I'm not sure how long it will take. Besides," he added, laughing, "now that I've seen how your roommate sleeps, I wouldn't worry about the phone waking her up."

When he had gone, promising again to call her later, Hailey checked one more time to make sure Nell was breathing and then went to the window to gather her thoughts before an hour or two of trying, somehow, to study.

She reached the window just in time to see

Finn board one of the shuttles. As it pulled away, she could clearly see the sign on the front, announcing its destination.

The sign read DOWNTOWN.

Downtown? Finn had said he was going to the library.

Where was he going? And why had he lied to her?

Maybe he had an errand in town that he'd forgotten about. But . . . it was late. Everything in town was closed.

It made no sense. Finn had clearly said he had some research to do, and was going to the library.

He had . . . lied.

People lied to hide things. What was Finn hiding from her? And why did he feel he had to?

Hailey closed her eyes and leaned against the window. If she couldn't trust Finn . . . the thought made her sick.

But . . . she really didn't know that much about Finn, did she? Not really. She couldn't even be positive about where he *lived*.

Hailey stood at the window a few more seconds before making up her mind. The shuttle would be making numerous stops. If she hurried . . .

On her way out, she stopped at Amy's door

to ask if Amy would be willing to study in room 416, so that Nell wouldn't be alone. "After everything that's happened," she said apologetically as Amy obligingly collected her books, "I'd just feel better if there were *two* people in that room."

Amy understood and said, "No problem."

Then Hailey hurried outside to her car.

As expected, a ticket for parking illegally had been thrust under her windshield wipers. It seemed unimportant. Hailey grabbed it, tossed it on the front seat and jumped in after it.

Then she started the engine, backed up, and turned the car around to follow the shuttle bus. And Finn.

# Chapter 19

Hailey caught up with the shuttle as it was passing through Twin Falls. Several students disembarked at the stone bridge in the center of town. Finn wasn't among them.

Finn got off at the Fourth Street corner.

He was headed for Darlene's house.

Hailey felt a wash of shame at what she was doing. Spying on Finn! If he saw her, how would she ever explain?

I couldn't, she told herself. What would I say? It was such a nice night, Finn, I decided to take a ride. It *wasn't* a nice night. It was cold, moonless, and damp. And wouldn't Finn think it was weird that she'd leave Nell alone when, just a little while ago, she'd thrown such a fit about Nell being in danger? Of course he would.

She didn't want him to know that she'd been following him . . . that she didn't trust him completely. I'm getting as paranoid as Nell, she thought in disgust. Finn probably just changed his mind about going to the library. And there I was, jumping to the conclusion that he was lying. *What* is wrong with me?

Still, how could she be expected to trust *anyone* after everything that had happened?

But Finn wasn't just anyone.

Deciding, Hailey pulled her car into a driveway and turned around. If she couldn't trust Finn, she didn't want to know it. Because she couldn't deal with it. No way.

As she steered away from Fourth Street, she couldn't help glancing in her rearview mirror. She saw Finn running up the steps to Darlene's house.

He must be looking for Darlene again. Maybe he'd heard that she was back.

Then, remembering Nell's dire thoughts about Darlene's brother, Hailey slammed on the brakes in the middle of the street. Finn was probably looking for Darlene . . . but what if he found Mike there instead? If Nell was right, Mike Riggs could be a vicious killer.

Then the front door of the Riggs house opened, and Hailey saw silhouetted in the doorway the figure of Darlene's mother.

She sagged in relief against the back of the

seat. Finn was perfectly safe with Darlene's parents in the house.

Besides, she reminded herself as she resumed driving, Finn wouldn't be on that list of people who had hurt Darlene, or encouraged her in her pursuit of Robert Q. Finn hadn't done either one.

But she knew she wouldn't be able to sleep until Finn called and said he was safely back at Lester.

"Finn called," Amy told Hailey when she entered room 416. "He couldn't believe you weren't here." Amy's brows furrowed. "Was I not supposed to tell him you'd gone out? You didn't tell me not to."

Hailey shook her head. "No, it's okay. I'll explain tomorrow." Although she had no idea what she'd say.

Amy picked up her books. Glancing toward Nell's bed, she said with envy, "Boy, I wish I could sleep like that! She never *moved*." Then she said more seriously, "Hailey, I think Finn thought you were with another guy. I could hear it in his voice."

"Another guy?"

"After I told him you weren't here, at first he sounded worried. But when I told him you were fine, his voice got all stiff and all he said was, Never mind, I'll see her tomorrow. But he sounded upset."

Now he wouldn't call when he got back to Lester. And when she *did* talk to him, where was she going to tell him she'd been? "Oh, no place special, Finn, I was just following you."

I don't *think* so, she told herself grimly. She thanked Amy, closed and locked the door behind her, propped the chair under the doorknob, and went to bed.

But unlike Nell, who slumbered away peacefully, Hailey lay awake for hours.

Hailey's first thought upon awakening the next morning was, I have to see Finn and find out if he talked to Mike Riggs last night. Or Darlene, if she was back. But if she called Lester, that twit at the desk would say, "No Conran here."

The truth was, she was nervous about seeing Finn. Amy had said Finn sounded annoyed, and it was going to be impossible to explain to him where she'd been. Maybe it would be a good idea to avoid him until she could figure out what to say.

Her second thought was, I need to find out if Darlene is back. If she is, who better to ask about Mike Riggs?

Nell had already left for her run. Glancing

at her jumbled bedding, Hailey remembered the terror of the night before . . . thinking Nell was . . . dead. Her hands began to shake. She had trouble combing her hair.

She had to find out something. They couldn't go on like this.

When Hailey called the Riggs house, Darlene's mother answered.

"I was just wondering," Hailey said, "if Darlene had come home."

"Oh, no, not yet," she was told. "In a few days, we're hoping."

Hailey hated to hang up. This phone line was her link to Mike Riggs. Impulsively, she added, "Well, is Mike there?"

"No, I'm sorry, he's not."

Well, at least she hadn't said, "Mike who?" the way everyone on campus seemed to.

"He does live at home, doesn't he?"

"Oh, of course. But he had an early class."

"Would you by any chance know what class he has?"

"Let me check his schedule. It's right here."

Hailey heard the phone dropping, and the rustling of paper. Then Mrs. Riggs came back on the line. "Here it is. A nine o'clock philosophy class. Professor Monahan. Lindbergh Hall, Room 132."

That was helpful, but it wasn't enough! She

would have to lie, a little. No other choice. "Mrs. Riggs, the thing is, I have some things Darlene left in my room. I thought she might want them. I can give them to Mike, but I've had trouble finding him on campus, and I don't know what he looks like. Does he look like Darlene?"

"Oh, no," Mrs. Riggs said, "Michael looks just like his father. He's very handsome. And if it helps, he wore his blue sweater today, the one I knitted for his birthday."

Like his father? Hailey had met Darlene's father the night of the pizza party. A small, weary-looking man with graying hair. Handsome? I guess that's true love, she thought. But it was hard to imagine a younger version of Mr. Riggs.

She thanked Darlene's mother and hung up. Then she dressed in jeans and her gray Salem sweatshirt under a navy blue blazer. Making sure she had her key, she hurried off to Lindbergh Hall.

She only had to wait five minutes outside of room 132 before the door opened and students began pouring into the hall. She saw no one who resembled Mr. Riggs. Ian and Milo were in the class, Robert Q and Lyle, and Finn and Pete, but room 132 must have been cold because they were all wearing their jackets. No blue sweater was visible. None of them saw Hailey half-hidden behind the open door, and she let them hurry on to their next class without calling to them. She had to concentrate on finding Mike Riggs.

When she peered inside the room, it was empty except for the teacher, stuffing papers into his briefcase.

Had she missed Mike Riggs? Or had he cut class? Would someone actually hurry from town to campus practically at the crack of dawn and then skip the class they'd come for? That seemed irrational.

Hailey uttered a short laugh. Irrational? She could be dealing with a murderer here. Irrational seemed too mild a term.

If Mike Riggs hadn't attended class, where *was* he? Hailey thought of Nell, running alone in the woods, and fought panic. She couldn't get upset about Nell again, when her roommate was probably perfectly safe.

And, as if she were being rewarded for thinking so sensibly, the first person she saw when she left Lindbergh Hall was Nell. She was standing beside the fountain in the Commons talking to Pete.

Hailey hurried over to them. The wind stung her cheeks. The sun that had been shining when she first left Devereaux had taken refuge behind thick gray clouds that hinted at more snow, and the air had turned raw and chilly.

"Gotta go!" Nell cried as Hailey arrived. "Catch you later."

"I heard about your scare last night," Pete said, watching Nell run in the direction of the dorm. He was hatless, his blond hair tousled, his ears beet-red. "Should she be running in the woods by herself?"

"I was wondering the same thing this morning," Hailey said, sitting down on the low stone wall around the fountain. "But I have a feeling that unless we tied her feet to the bed and locked Nell in, she'd run no matter what was going on."

Pete laughed. "You're right."

"Listen, Pete," Hailey said, "I'm getting really suspicious about Mike Riggs."

Pete sat down beside her, stomping his feet on the old, hardened snow to keep them warm. "Mike Riggs?"

"Darlene's brother."

"Her brother?"

"Yes. What everyone who was hurt . . . or killed . . . had in common is *Darlene*. At first, I thought it was *her*. But she really is in Willowcreek, so . . ."

Pete looked shocked. "Darlene wouldn't hurt anyone."

"I know. But she was having a really hard time dealing with the Robert Q stuff. I thought maybe she'd flipped. But now I'm wondering about her brother. Couldn't he be angry enough about what happened to her to seek revenge *for* her?"

"What about that guy she was dating? He looked like he could get really nasty. That Jessup guy."

"The police said Bo wasn't in town when some of the stuff happened. Look, help me out here, okay? Do you know Mike Riggs?"

"Mike Riggs? You don't think it was Bo?" Pete rubbed his hands together.

"Oh, Pete, I don't know *what* I think anymore. I just know I'm tired of looking over my shoulder all the time. Richard's dead and I came close, and other people have been hurt . . . and someone's getting away with it. I'm scared. So is Nell."

Pete said he didn't know Mike Riggs, but he'd find out what he could and get back to her. And then, complaining that he was freezing, he left.

Hailey was cold, too. But she stayed where she was for a few more minutes. Campus seemed so . . . normal. People hurried, heads down against the wind, to and from buildings just as they always did. Small groups gathered here and there, chatting briefly before rushing off to find warmth. Except for a trio of town police who glanced inquiringly at Hailey as they passed, campus looked pretty much the way it was supposed to.

Then why, Hailey asked herself as she stood up, am I so terrified?

Because, came the answer, appearances can be deceiving.

# Chapter 20

Hailey was within a few yards of Devereaux when Milo Keith caught up with her. It occurred to her that maybe Milo could help. She waved him inside the dorm to escape the cold. The lobby was crowded with uniformed marching band members about to leave for a pep rally. They were making so much noise, laughing, talking, tooting a few careless notes on trombones and trumpets, that Hailey couldn't hear Milo's answer to her question.

"Do you know Darlene's brother, Mike Riggs?" she shouted over the cacophony.

Milo moved into a corner to let the troupe pass by. "No. I never met him. But his name isn't Riggs."

A trombone on its way out the door blasted a trio of deep, resonating notes.

"What?" Hailey shouted as a drummer jostled her from behind. "What did you say?"

Milo leaned closer. "I said, Darlene's brother's name isn't *Riggs!*"

With a melodic tooting on a flute, the last band member left the lobby, and in the ensuing silence, Hailey caught Milo's answer.

"It's not? What *is* it?"

Milo shrugged bony shoulders. "Beats me. But we were talking about it after you and Finn left Duffy's in such a hurry last night. Our waiter heard us mention Darlene's name. He grew up near Darlene. We asked him about her brother, and he said Mike was really her half brother . . . his mom had married Darlene's dad. But Mike kept his original last name. So it's not Riggs."

Chagrin washed over Hailey. She'd been asking questions all over campus about someone who didn't exist? There *wasn't* any Mike Riggs?

Who, exactly, am I *looking* for? Hailey wondered. "Okay, that's *it!*" she cried. "It is time to go to the horse's mouth. I'm calling Darlene and I'm *not* letting her talk about Robert Q. She's going to tell me *who* and *where* her *brother* is!"

"Good thinking. Gotta go." Milo turned to leave. But before he yanked the door open, he added, "Listen, Kingman, just be careful out there, okay? One thing I've learned from living at Nightmare Hall is, you can't be *too* careful, okay?"

Hailey smiled a rueful smile. "Okay. Will do."

As she waited, with a handful of other students, for the elevator, Hailey picked nervously at her nails. Darlene's brother could be *anyone*.

The hallway was chilly and deserted, and when Hailey arrived at room 416, Nell wasn't home. She and the others were already at the bonfire and pep rally for tomorrow's football game, which was where Hailey planned to go as soon as she'd talked to Darlene.

She dropped her books and jacket on her bed and went straight to the phone. Dialing Darlene's grandmother's house in Willowcreek, she wondered if Finn would be at the pep rally. And she wondered if he was mad at her because he thought she'd been with some other guy the night before.

"Oh, Hailey," Darlene gushed when she learned who was calling her, "I'm so glad you called! You'll never guess who's here. *Bo!* It turns out he's been here in Willowcreek the whole time, staying with his aunt, and trying to get up enough nerve to apologize to me about the way he behaved at the Sigma Chi party."

"*What?*" Hailey said.

"Bo was afraid I'd never forgive him for his temper tantrum. He didn't even wait for me that night, after all. He was so ashamed, he just got in his truck and drove here."

So, the police had been right. Bo *hadn't* been in town when things started going haywire.

Darlene rushed on: "Even when Bo found out I was in Willowcreek, too, he was afraid to come see me right away. Isn't that silly? As if I wouldn't forgive Bo, the person I love most in the whole world."

Hailey's head was spinning. Since when was Bo Jessup the person Darlene Riggs loved most in the whole world? What about Robert Q?

"Darlene, slow down! You're talking too fast. I thought you were finished with Bo."

"I know, Hailey, but I was wrong. I can't believe I gave up Bo for that creep, Robert Q."

Hailey's eyes widened. That *creep*? Darlene had switched her devotion back to Bo? *That* was fast.

Speaking in the same high-pitched, breathless voice she'd used when talking about Robert Q in the past, Darlene went on, "Bo *hates* working in the garage, so he's going to quit, and we're going to take some courses together at Salem — he's so wonderful, Hailey, I can't stand to be away from him for even a single second — I make him call me first thing every morning and last thing at night . . ."

Hailey stopped listening. Darlene's switched heroes, she thought, but she's still using the same script. Woman overboard. She may not be a killer, but she sure could use some help. "That's great, Darlene," Hailey said weakly, when Darlene finally paused for a breath. At least Bo apparently felt the same way about Darlene. He wouldn't hurt her the way Robert Q had.

"You know, Hailey," Darlene confided in a calmer voice, "I was pretty bummed that Mike got to go to college and I didn't. Part of the reason I didn't study harder in high school was, I knew my parents couldn't afford to send me. And Mike had some money his father had left him. It wasn't a lot, but it was enough to get him started. I didn't even have *that*, and I knew my parents figured it wasn't as important for a girl to go. That really ticked me off."

It was the perfect opening for Hailey. "Darlene, you never told me Mike wasn't your . . . well, I mean, you didn't say he was your half brother."

"Oh, gosh, Hailey, I never think of Mike that way. He's been just like my real brother right from the very first day. I think he'd do anything for me. He was *so* mad when all that stuff happened with Robert Q."

Just *how* mad had Darlene's brother been?

Footsteps sounded outside in the hall. Nell coming home? The pep rally couldn't be over already.

Time to get some answers. "Darlene, what exactly *is* Mike's last name, anyway? I was going to look him up, find out if he'd heard from you, but of course I was looking for a Mike Riggs." Hailey laughed. "And now I know there *is* no such person."

The footsteps were getting closer, echoing hollowly in the empty hall. They were too heavy to be Nell's. She walked lightly, gracefully, always on an imaginary balance beam.

"You probably already *know* my brother," Darlene said. "He's a freshman, like you, and he knows a lot of people. He was at the Sigma Chi party that night, Hailey, and if things hadn't been so crazy, I'd have introduced you. I know you'd like each other."

The footsteps came to a halt just outside the door to room 416.

And fear began to creep up Hailey's spine. She was alone in the dorm and someone was standing on the other side of the door. What if it was the same person who had pushed her out the window?

If she had gone to the bonfire with Nell, she'd be safe in a crowd right now.

There was a sharp knock on the door.

But before Hailey opened it, she repeated her question to Darlene. "What is Mike's last name, Darlene?"

And Darlene answered, "Conran. My brother's name is Michael Finn Conran."

# Chapter 21

Hailey stood stock-still, her mouth open in shock. *Finn* was Darlene's brother? No. He would have *told* her.

"Of course," Darlene rattled on, "we still call him Mike at home, but he goes by Finn now. It was his dad's name. Hailey? Hailey, are you still there?"

Without saying good-bye, Hailey slowly, carefully, replaced the receiver on the wall telephone.

Finn was Darlene's brother.

No. Not possible. She had *talked* about Darlene with Finn. And not once had he said, "She's my sister." Not once.

But . . . Darlene certainly knew who her own *brother* was.

It had to be true.

Finn had deliberately kept from her the information that he and Darlene were related? Why would he *do* that?

Lost in disbelief, she was oblivious to the knocking on the door, until a voice shocked her back to reality by calling, "Hailey?"

Hailey jumped, startled.

Then the door opened a crack and Pete Torrance poked his head in. "I could hear you on the phone," he explained, "so I knew someone was in here. What's up? You look like you just lost your best friend."

"Oh, Pete, you scared me." Hailey's heart was pounding wildly.

"So, *did* you?" he persisted.

"Did I what?" She couldn't concentrate.

"I said, did you lose your best friend? Where *is* Nell, anyway?"

Maybe I *did* lose a best friend, Hailey thought sadly, but it wasn't Nell. Tears stung her eyelids.

Pete's voice changed. "Hailey, what's wrong? You look weird. It's not Nell, is it? Has something happened to Nell?"

"No, Nell's fine," Hailey answered in a surprisingly level voice. "She's probably already at the rally. I need to find her. Come on!"

Pete ran a hand through his unruly blond hair. "I'm not going anywhere until you tell me what's wrong."

Hailey told herself in desperation that hiding the truth about who he was didn't make Finn a killer. It *didn't*!

But . . . Finn was at the Sigma Chi party the night Gerrie was hit by the rock. And he was behind the frat house when Robert Q's car burned.

Darlene had said, "I think my brother would do anything for me."

*Anything?*

Hailey raised her eyes to meet Pete's worried gaze. Pete was Finn's friend. Maybe *he* could explain.

Please, please, she prayed, let him tell me that what I'm thinking is crazy, that his friend Finn isn't a liar and a killer. "We *have* to find Nell," she said urgently, grabbing Pete's hand. "We can talk while we look for her. C'mon!"

Together, they hurried down the hall to the elevator. She stabbed the down button. Then she turned to Pete and accused, "You *knew* there was no such person as Mike Riggs, didn't you? You sat right there on the fountain with me and played innocent. You even said you'd ask around, when you knew the whole time that Darlene's brother was Finn." The elevator arrived, the door opened, and they stepped inside. "How *could* you?" Hailey cried as the doors closed. "I feel *so* stupid. You *knew!*"

Pete's face flushed guiltily. "I'm sorry, Hailey. I really am. But I'd promised Finn I wouldn't tell anyone."

"*Why?* Is he ashamed of his own sister?" But even before Pete answered, Hailey knew it wasn't that simple. It couldn't be.

"That's not why. But . . . you might *wish* it was, when I tell you what I think." The elevator doors slid open and they exited to an empty lobby. Pete held the heavy front door open. A bitter gust of wind greeted them. Darkness had fallen while they were inside. From the wide stone steps of Devereaux, Hailey and Pete could see the orange glow of the huge bonfire in a field behind Butler Hall, and hear the marching band playing a rousing rendition of the school fight song.

Pete hunched his green-jacketed shoulders against the cold. "Finn *said* he didn't want anyone to know he was Darlene's brother because he intended to nose around, find out who had thrown that rock at Gerrie. Darlene was already a suspect, so he *said* no one would tell him anything if they knew he was her brother. Made sense to me. Then, when you were pushed out the window, he said it would be safer for you if *you* didn't know. So I kept quiet, and when you asked me about Darlene's brother, I pretended I didn't know who he was. For *your* sake, Hailey."

I don't want to hear this, Hailey told herself. And I should be thinking of Nell. She's still on the list of a murderer. She might not be safe even in a crowd.

Tugging on Pete's hand, she said anxiously, "We're wasting time. Talk while we walk."

They broke into a fast lope toward Butler Hall. "It never crossed my mind," Pete said, "that *Finn* might have thrown that rock, because he was furious over the way Darlene was treated at that party."

Hailey tensed, but didn't break her stride. Finn had thrown that rock? No. Pete was wrong. He *had* to be!

"Finn wouldn't have," was all she said.

"That's what I thought, at first," Pete responded. "But . . ."

They passed the library, open and well-lit but looking nearly deserted through the wide windows. No one wanted to burrow into research books when they could be having fun at a bonfire.

"But what?"

"Remember the day Richard was killed?" Pete asked.

She would never forget it. "Of course I do. Why?"

"Well, Finn and I got off the shuttle at the diner, remember?"

"So did Robert Q," Hailey reminded him.

"Yeah, but Robert Q *stayed* there. Finn *didn't*."

That stopped Hailey in her tracks. She fought the urge to clap her hands over her ears. "Finn *left* the diner?"

"Twenty minutes after we got there. I heard him telling Caesar he had an emergency at home. The next thing I knew, he was running out of the diner just in time to grab a shuttle downtown. Never even told me he was leaving."

The laughter and shouting from the bonfire made it hard for Hailey to hear Pete. He had to shout.

But then, Hailey thought, I don't want to hear what he's telling me anyway. "Why didn't you tell the police, when they were asking all those questions on campus, that Finn left the diner? Why didn't Caesar tell them?"

"Caesar's old. He probably forgot. And I wasn't going to rat on Finn. Anyway, it never crossed my mind that Finn could have killed Richard, or that he'd gone anywhere near the mall. I figured he *did* have an emergency. His grandmother's illness could have gotten worse, or Darlene could have come unglued because of Robert Q. When I asked Finn about it later, he said it was family stuff."

Hailey turned and began walking again, yanking Pete along with her, but urging him to keep talking. They reached the outside edges of the celebrating throng. She had to hold Pete's hand tightly, and he had to shout to make himself heard. "Finn hated Richard for agreeing to take Darlene home from the party, for money."

Hailey had to elbow her way through the crowd, dragging Pete with her. Her eyes searched for Nell's orange jacket. "Finn knew about that?"

"Yes, and he was furious. I'd never seen him so mad."

"There!" Hailey cried, pointing. "There's Nell, over there with Ann and Amy, and Ian and Jess." Her knees went weak with relief. "Finn isn't with them."

"Well, I could have told you Finn wasn't here," Pete yelled over an ear-pounding drum roll. "He's at home."

Hailey looked up at him as someone jostled her from behind. "Why didn't you *tell* me?" she shouted.

"You didn't ask. I thought you were looking for Nell."

"Well, I was. But now that I know she's safe, I want to see Finn. I want him to tell me for himself why he didn't tell me the truth . . . that he was Darlene's brother and that he didn't live on campus." She was being pushed between two groups of pushing, shouting revellers. "Let's get out of here."

They elbowed their way back to the fringes of the noisy crowd. When they had broken free, Hailey turned to Pete. "How do you know Finn is home?"

"He called me. Said he had work to do in his darkroom and wasn't coming up for the rally."

A soft moan escaped Hailey's lips. "God, I feel so *stupid*! All that time, I thought he lived at Lester."

"That's just where he picks up the shuttle. Look, not telling you where he lives seems kind of . . . trivial, don't you think? I hate to say this, but I really believe that Finn went to the mall and ran Richard down. It's the only explanation that makes any sense. And it explains a *lot*."

A sudden gust of icy wind assaulted them. Hailey pulled her knit cap further down around her ears. She couldn't be sure if she did it to keep out the cold . . . or the sound of Pete's voice.

The music behind them ended. Loud applause and shouting took its place. Hailey couldn't understand how so many people could be having so much fun when Pete had just told her that he thought Finn Conran had deliberately killed Richard Wentworth.

"There's more, Hailey," Pete added somberly. "The day you were pushed out the window, Finn wasn't *with* us when Nell and I got to Devereaux. We ran into him upstairs, in the hall outside your room. He said he'd just come off the other elevator, but I think now he was lying. I think he'd just come from your room."

It was too much for Hailey. She felt dizzy, disoriented. She could feel herself weaving, tilting, as if the earth were spinning beneath her.

Seeing her distress, Pete put a steadying arm around her shoulders. "I think he just flipped, Hailey. Studying, working at the diner, and then all that stuff happening to Darlene, it was too much for Finn. He lost it." He reached down to tilt her chin up toward him. "We have to call the police, Hailey."

"No . . ."

"Yes. I don't like the idea any more than you do, but we don't have any choice."

"I'm going down there," she said suddenly, pulling away from Pete. "To Finn's. I have to talk to him. I want him to tell me the truth. I *have* to hear it from him."

"Okay, but you're not going alone. And I'm calling the cops first, okay? There's a pay phone in the library. I'll use that." He glanced down at her as they began walking. "You okay?"

"No," she said, her teeth chattering with cold and fear, "I'm not."

But she kept walking.

# Chapter 22

Hailey waited in the library lobby while Pete called the police. She heard him giving the address on Fourth Street. Her head began to throb. It felt like two giant hands were squeezing it. Any second now, it would explode, like an overripe melon.

"The cops were already planning to pick him up," Pete said when he'd hung up. "Caesar remembered that Finn left the diner the day Richard was killed. The desk sergeant said they're getting a warrant now. You still want to see him?"

"Yes." Hailey's lips felt numb. "Take me down there."

She let Pete lead her to his car. She moved stiffly, a silent robot.

"I blame myself," Pete said quietly as they sped toward town, the river on their right. "I knew Finn was stressed to the max. College was too important to him, you know? He had to work for a year to add to the money his father left him, and when he finally got here, he wanted it to be perfect. He knocked himself out, trying. And it was working. He was doing great. But then all that stuff happened with Darlene. He couldn't stand seeing her get hurt. And I wasn't paying enough attention to how really angry he was. Anyway, I was so sure it was Bo. I'm sorry, Hailey."

"It's not your fault. I didn't notice anything, either. I thought he was fine." *So* fine, she thought unhappily. She uttered a short, bitter laugh. "I thought our bad guy was just about everyone on campus *but* Finn. I guess, like Darlene, I'm not a very good judge of character." Quiet tears slid down her cheeks, and she fell silent.

Realizing that she couldn't talk about it anymore, Pete concentrated on driving.

Hailey made her mind a blank. It was the only way to keep from screaming.

When Pete pulled the car to a stop in Twin Falls at 1006 Fourth Street, no police cars had arrived. The house was dark, with only a faint glow reflected from a rear window.

"He said he'd be working in the darkroom," Pete reminded Hailey, "in the basement."

Hailey's heart began skidding around in her

chest, out of control. Her hands trembled, her legs barely made it up the cement steps to the porch. "I can't go in there," she whispered as Pete stooped to unearth a key from under a mat. "Maybe we should wait for the police."

"If we wait for them," Pete said, unlocking the door and pushing it open, "you won't get a chance to talk to Finn yourself. Isn't that what you want?"

It *was*. She wanted to look straight into Finn's brown eyes and ask him why he had lied to her. She *needed* that.

She followed Pete into the darkened house.

"The darkroom is downstairs," Pete said again, taking Hailey's hand.

She hung back. "Pete . . ."

"It's okay. I know my way around. And Hailey . . ." He stopped, turned toward her in the dark and bent to kiss her cheek, startling her. "I won't let anything bad happen. Nell would never forgive me if I let Finn hurt either one of us."

Hailey wanted to scream, "Finn would never hurt me!" But she couldn't. Because Nell and Pete had met Finn in the fourth floor hall at Devereaux the day she'd been pushed out of the window . . . and Finn shouldn't have *been* there. He didn't live at Devereaux and he hadn't been visiting her *or* Pete.

It was time to face the truth. She'd been wrong about Finn from the beginning. *Very* wrong.

Pete opened the basement door and flicked a switch that illuminated a flight of narrow, enclosed wooden stairs leading downward.

Hailey stared at them. Finn was down there, unaware that his life was about to change forever.

She followed Pete down the stairs.

The room they entered was wide, square, with a low, white-tiled ceiling and walls panelled in a dark wood that matched the tile squares on the floor. A worn plaid couch and two matching chairs lined one wall. A television set on a rolling metal cart sat against the opposite wall. The rear end of the room was full of weight-lifting equipment. But it was a bar at the other end of the room that caught Hailey's eyes. The bar was cluttered with framed pictures.

She let go of Pete's hand and walked over to look at the photos. They were family pictures: Darlene as a baby, Darlene's father and stepmother's wedding photo, and Darlene and a boy, clearly her new brother. And there were pictures of Finn, as a young teenager, looking much too serious.

Tears filled Hailey's eyes again. He couldn't

have had an easy life, she thought. Moving into a new family when he was young, never having much money, working so hard to get to college . . .

If I had come down here the night of Darlene's pizza party, she thought, I would have known then that Finn was Darlene's brother. But . . . would that really have changed anything?

Probably not. She never would have suspected Finn of throwing that rock. Not then. It was hard enough thinking it now, when she knew it was true.

Wiping her eyes with her jacket sleeve, she turned away from the pictures. And noticed a bare red bulb protruding from the wall over a narrow door off to her left. The dark room. But the bulb wasn't on.

"Shouldn't that red light be on?" she asked Pete. "If Finn is working in there, isn't that light supposed to warn people to stay out?"

"Probably burned out," he said, moving to the end of the room where the weight-lifting equipment was stationed. "Finn forgets about stuff like that. He's got a lot on his mind, our Finn has." Slipping out of his jacket, he reached down and picked up a black dumbbell. Although it was small, it looked very heavy. But Pete picked it up easily. "Go ahead and knock."

Hailey took a deep breath, marched resolutely over to the darkroom door, and rapped sharply. Once, twice . . .

There was no answer from inside.

Frowning, Hailey turned around. "I don't think he's here."

Pete grinned at her. "Well, that's okay. We're here. You and me. Excuse me, you and *I*." He glanced lazily around the room. "Kind of cozy down here, am I right?"

With his cheeks still red with cold, his clear, blue eyes shining, his broad shoulders straining only slightly under a plaid shirt as he raised and lowered the heavy weight, Pete looked, Hailey decided, like the cover of a fitness magazine.

But . . . there was something very wrong with his smile.

"Pete?" Hailey could sense the ominous feeling descending upon her, heavy and threatening. "Where is Finn?"

The grin remained in place, as if it had been painted on. "Gee, Hailey, how should *I* know? *I* don't keep track of Finn Conran's comings and goings. But *I* figure, wherever he is . . . probably at the bonfire looking for *you* . . . he'll be home soon. Finn's one of those boring people who needs a good night's sleep." Pete hefted the dumbbell again, this time aiming it slightly in Hailey's direction. "And when he does walk in, he's going to find you on this nice fake wood floor with your skull bashed in."

Frozen in place, Hailey stared at him.

Pete laughed. And said, "Surprise, surprise!"

# Chapter 23

Hailey, her eyes on Pete, backed up against the darkroom door. "What's the matter with you? That's not funny, Pete!"

Laughing, he moved to block the narrow entrance to the stairway, the basement's only exit. The heavy dumbbell was still in his hand. "Oh, *I* think it is. I think it's hilarious that you're here, alone with me." His eyes glittering with amusement, he said, "And you thought you were stupid *before*? You must be feeling like a total moron right about now."

"You?" she whispered, "It was *you*?"

He nodded smugly.

"It wasn't Finn?"

A laugh of derision burst from Pete. "Finn? Are you kidding? He was furious about what happened to Darlene. But when I asked him what he was going to do about it, all he said was, he was going to find out who really threw that rock."

So that part of it had been true, at least. Relief that Finn wasn't a killer disappeared quickly as Hailey realized that she was alone in the basement with someone who *was*.

Pete's lip curled in contempt for Finn. "Some protective older brother! If he'd *really* cared about Darlene, he'd have done what *I* did."

"*You* stole my purse at the mall," Hailey said through lips stiff with fear. "And made a copy of the key. My purse was never turned in. You had it the whole time."

"Well, you're so *careless*, Hailey! Leaving your purse hanging on your chair like that. You *deserved* to have it stolen." Pete sat down on the bottom step, and turned sideways to lean back against the wall and watch Hailey. He continued to curl the dumbbell as he talked. "I had to hide that stupid purse inside my jacket when I walked into Devereaux. But even without it, I'd have found a way to get a key. If not yours, then Nell's."

"And you didn't *need* a key when you trashed our room, because I hadn't locked the door." Anger stiffening her backbone, Hailey drew herself up to her full height. "I *knew* Finn couldn't have done that. Not that . . ."

"Oh, you *did* not," Pete countered with a sneer. "Not five minutes ago, you thought he did it *all*. You bought my story, hook, line, and sinker. I could see it in your face."

Hailey's cheeks burned. "You . . . you never called the police, did you?"

"Well, of *course* not, Hailey. That would be pretty stupid. And as you must have figured out by now, stupid is one thing I'm not." Pete smiled. "Or you wouldn't *be* here, *would* you?"

Stung, Hailey shot back, "At least I'm not a murderer!"

Anger darkened Pete's eyes. "I never intended to kill Richard. I was only going to steal his stupid car and push it into the river. He deserved far worse than that for the way he treated Darlene. The jerk jumped right in front of the car and wouldn't move. He thought I was *playing*, the idiot!" Pete sighed, a sound of self-pity. "Wasn't my fault," he muttered. "But," he added cheerfully, "with *him* dead, it didn't matter what I did after that, right? Nothing more to lose."

Hailey was only half-listening. Behind her back one hand closed around the darkroom's doorknob. Her eyes searched frantically for a way out . . . a window, another door . . . there was nothing. The darkroom wouldn't have an exit . . . unless it had a window . . .

"You're looking a little pale, Hailey. Maybe you ought to sit down."

Hailey ignored him. She remained standing. She wasn't moving one step away from the door.

"Aren't you going to ask me how I knew where Finn kept the house key?" Pete asked her in a sly voice. "Come on, Hailey, get with it! You can't expect to get information if you're not willing to ask the questions."

"How did you know about the key?" she asked through numb lips.

"Glad you asked. The truth is, I grew up two blocks away from here. When I graduated from high school, my parents moved to Florida. No great loss. I moved into Devereaux. But growing up, I spent almost as much time in this house as Finn and Darlene did." Pete's face darkened. "And there, as Shakespeare says, lies the rub. Darlene thought of me as another brother. And believe me, that wasn't the way I *wanted* her to think of me."

Hailey, thoroughly frightened, was having trouble digesting Pete's words. "You did it all? You threw that rock at Gerrie and burned Robert Q's car? You framed Puffy and Susan and pushed me out of the window? *Why?*"

The question infuriated him. He jumped to

his feet, his eyes blazing. His face was flushed, and he shook with rage. "Don't you understand *anything*?" he shouted. "Aren't you *listening* to me? I *loved* her!"

Frightened by the sudden change in him, Hailey shrank back against the door, tightening her grip on the doorknob behind her. "Who?" she asked, bewildered. "Who did you love? I thought you and Nell . . ."

Pete stomped one foot on the wooden tile floor. "Nell? *Nell?*" he screamed, his eyes bulging. "Nell is a *nothing* compared to Darlene!"

"You . . . you were in love with Darlene?" Hailey whispered. "Darlene Riggs?"

"Of *course* Darlene Riggs," Pete said with a contemptuous sneer. "I've been crazy about her for years. But, like I *said* when you weren't *listening*, she saw me as a buddy, and that's all. And even that ended when she started dating. Never *me*," he added bitterly. "She just laughed when I asked her. Thought I was kidding. She dated two or three guys before that jerk, Bo, came along . . . but never *me*. After she met him, she hardly knew I was alive. But I never got her off my mind. Then she took up with that creep, Robert Q. And he *hurt* her!" Pete's voice rose. "He treated Darlene like dirt!" he cried. "They *all* did!"

"That look on your face," Hailey said, her

hand behind her back slowly turning the door-knob, "that first night at the diner, when Darlene met Robert Q. I thought it was disgust. But it wasn't, was it? It was . . . you were furious at what was happening between them." Please, please, she prayed, don't let this door be locked!

"I wasn't mad at *her*," Pete said with scorn. "It wasn't Darlene's fault. Every time Darlene meets a guy, she falls like a ton of bricks. That's just the way she is. I understood, but I knew she'd get hurt, sooner or later. And I swore," his mouth tightened grimly, "that whoever did the hurting would pay."

The doorknob turned all the way. Gently, gently, Hailey tugged. She could feel the door give slightly, telling her it wasn't locked.

"They *talked* about her," Pete ranted. He began marching rapidly back and forth in front of Hailey, curling the dumbbell up, down, up, down. "They made fun of her, laughed at her, as if she wasn't *worth* anything. Someone had to stop them. Someone had to *punish* them." When he glared angrily at Hailey, she was amazed to see tears shining in his eyes. "I thought if she knew I'd made them pay, she'd love me then, but before I could *tell* her, she was back with Bo again."

"I'm not sorry I did what I did," he said

harshly. "Even if Darlene doesn't love me. They all deserved it."

"I didn't," Hailey said. "I never hurt Darlene. Why did you push me out that window?"

Pete shook his head. "You and that stupid roommate of yours *encouraged* her. I was in the hall that day when she came to your room. She looked so excited. She said you were going to help her." Talking about it increased Pete's anger. Hailey's fear grew, watching his movements increase in intensity until every step he took, back and forth, pounded into the tile like a hammer. That's the way he's going to pound my skull with that dumbbell, she thought.

"She was doing it all for Robert Q!" he shouted. "With *your* help." Then, more quietly, he added, almost to himself, "She'd be really mad if she knew I pushed you. But," more cheerfully, "she's not *going* to know, *is* she? I never planned to tell her that part of it. And now, everyone's going to think Finn did it." He smiled. "That Finn did *all* of it. Darlene's so hung up on Bo now, it wouldn't do me any good to tell her I'm the one who got even with those creeps for her. So why should I go to jail? Let Finn go. The cops will think you two had a lover's quarrel when you found out he lied to you. I'll testify." He looked very pleased with himself. "I'll say that I'm the one who *told* you the truth about Finn. Because I *am*, right? So I won't be lying on the witness stand."

Hailey listened carefully to his words. He was telling her she wasn't going to leave the basement alive.

Still pacing, Pete glanced toward the tired-looking plaid sofa. "Finn hangs out down here a lot. Working in the darkroom, watching TV. He should be home soon. He'll get a glass of milk from the fridge and come on down here. And guess what he'll find?" Pete grinned. "You! Only . . . only maybe he'll have a hard time recognizing you by then."

Hailey's grip tightened on the doorknob. There wouldn't be a way out of the darkroom, but the door should lock from the inside. Still, Pete looked strong. Was he strong enough to break down a wooden door?

She would have to take that chance. It was better than no chance at all.

Finn, she prayed, come *home*!

Pete put a finger to his lips and stood still for a second, thinking. Then he murmured, "And Nell's punishment will be knowing you're dead."

Hoisting the dumbbell above his head, he moved toward Hailey. A sickening, determined look spread across his square, handsome face.

Now! Hailey yanked the darkroom door

open, whirled, and darted inside, slamming the door shut in Pete's face. Fumbling in the dark for the lock, her fingers found a button on the inside knob. She pushed it in and backed away from the door, her breath coming in short, painful gasps.

On the other side of the door, an enraged Pete screamed her name.

# Chapter 24

Pete's screams of rage assaulted Hailey's ears. A vicious kick shook the cheap wooden door.

That door won't keep him out for very long, Hailey realized.

The darkroom seemed to be little more than a closet. A narrow space, a low ceiling, no windows. As Hailey backed away from the door, something brushed against her face. A string . . . a light pull? She yanked on it, and the narrow little space took on a soft reddish glow. There were shelves on her left, crammed with photography supplies, a sink on her right with a cabinet underneath it.

"Hailey! Get *out* here! *Now!*" The scream was high-pitched, a shrill, frantic sound that turned Hailey's blood to ice. When she didn't reply, there was a brief moment of silence and then Pete screamed her name again and slammed something heavy against the door. It shook under the force of the blow.

With the second blow, the wood began to splinter.

The dumbbell, Hailey thought, taking another step backward. He's breaking the door down with the same dumbbell he's planning to use to smash my skull.

Her eyes frantically scanned the rosy-glowing darkroom for a weapon . . . something she could use to save her life.

The door was bending, breaking, under the repeated blows. She had so little time . . .

"I *hate* you!" Pete screamed as he hammered away at the door. "I hate *all* of you! Darlene wasn't dating Bo anymore. I might have had a chance with her." He began sobbing, his breath coming in ragged gasps. "If Robert Q hadn't come along. They all . . . thought it was so funny . . . Robert Q sweeping a town girl off her feet. And . . . and *you* helped, Hailey . . . you and Nell. You ruined any chance I had of making Darlene love me!"

The middle of the door was bending inward, the wood splitting, cracking right before Hailey's eyes.

She could find nothing to use as a weapon. The shelves were crammed full, but she saw no knife, no hammer, no scissors, nothing to defend herself with. Nothing but . . .

Chemicals! In fat, squat black and yellow jugs. They were lined up neatly under the bottom shelf on her left. Three, no four, jugs. In the dim, rosy glow she could see a warning printed in large letters on the front of the jugs. Meaning the jugs were full of something dangerous. Dangerous . . . that was what she needed . . .

"I'm going . . . to get you, Hailey," Pete gasped. "You can't get away now. You should have . . . minded your own . . . business." He grunted with the effort of delivering another solid blow to the splintering door. "I'm almost there, Hailey!" he called gaily. "And then . . . and then you're . . . going to . . . die!" Another cackling laugh before he set to work on the door again.

Pete's repeated blows had created an inch-wide opening in the center of the door. She had only seconds left.

Hailey crouched near the bottom shelf, grabbed a jug, forced her shaking hands to unscrew its cap and, clutching the heavy jug, stood up. She realized immediately that the jug's neck was too narrow. The contents would spill out too slowly to do any good.

A pail . . . she needed a pail . . . something with a wide mouth.

"I fixed Robert Q," Pete muttered loudly

between blows. "I fixed *all* of them! They deserved it! They got what was coming to them. And now, Hailey, it's *your* turn. You won't get away this time. Not . . . this . . . time!"

There! Under the sink, a wide plastic bin, like a dishpan. Hailey grabbed it and dumped half the contents of the jug into the wide, open bin and lifted it up with both hands.

Then she turned and, holding the bin out in front of her like a gift, faced the door.

"If you'd stayed out of it," Pete shouted, "I could have made her love me. I *could* have!"

"You can't *make* someone love you!" Hailey shouted back. Pieces of wood flew, and the hole in the door's middle widened. "People only love other people if they *want* to!" She could see most of Pete's face now. His eyes were wild, crazed, his face soaked with sweat from his hammering.

"Shut *up!*" he screamed, baring his teeth. One powerful hand reached in through the jagged hole in the door and turned the inside knob, releasing the lock.

Trembling violently, scarcely breathing, Hailey hoisted the bin higher. The liquid sloshed dangerously close to the edges. Careful, careful, she cautioned silently . . . if you spill it on your hands, it'll burn and you'll drop the bin. And then you're lost.

"Here I *co-ome*," Pete singsonged happily, and shoved the battered, broken door open. When he was on the threshold, he grinned at Hailey. "Hi, honey, I'm home."

Hailey waited only long enough to see the wicked dumbbell held high, ready to crash down upon her head. Then, taking a deep, ragged breath, she flung the contents of the bin directly into Pete's face.

The dumbbell thudded to the floor as Pete's hands flew to his face. He staggered backward, screaming, a terrible, anguished sound that echoed throughout the basement.

Hailey shuddered and closed her eyes. A sob of horror escaped her lips.

When she opened her eyes, Pete had staggered away from the doorway. His hands still at his face, he was lurching blindly about the basement. The screams had changed to horrible, guttural sounds of agony.

Hailey darted through the doorway, slipped around the corner and raced up the stairs. When she reached the top, she whirled to slam the door behind her and lock it. For added safety, she pulled a heavy table against the door.

"Hail-*ey*!" Pete screamed from the basement, "Hailey, *help* me!"

Ignoring the shout, she ran into the living

room to locate a telephone. When she found it, she dialed 911. Assured that the police and the ambulance were on the way, she hung up and left the house, gulping in fresh, cold air as she closed the front door behind her. Then her knees gave out, and she sank to the porch floor, leaning against the house. Pete's shouts were no longer audible, and the cold, damp air was a relief.

It amazed her that there were lights shining in nearly every house on the street. There were people in those houses, getting children ready for bed, watching television, doing homework . . . and they had no idea what had just gone on at 1006. She had almost died. And no one knew that yet but her . . . and Pete.

Poor Pete.

The trembling stopped.

She saw Finn coming down the street at the same moment that she heard the first faint sound of the sirens. Would the two of them have a moment alone before the police arrived? They had things they had to talk about. He hadn't told her the truth about who he was, even if it was to protect first Darlene, and then her. And she had suspected him of murder. They would have to sort those things out. It wouldn't be easy, and it would take time.

She watched him approach, loving the way

he moved . . . always hurrying, always eager to get to the next place. His hair looked almost black at night and it blew carelessly in the night breeze. She watched him brush it back impatiently as he neared the house, and she imagined the look in his brown-green eyes when he saw her there, tear-stained, her blazer dangling crazily around her shoulders, her hair wild.

The sirens grew louder, came closer, and people began appearing in doorways and at windows.

We will work it out, Hailey thought, Finn and I. While Pete gets the help he needs, Finn and I will take the time to work it out.

Hailey stood up.

# About the Author

"Writing tales of horror makes it hard to convince people that I'm a nice, gentle person," says **Diane Hoh**.

"So what's a nice woman like me doing scaring people?"

"Discovering the fearful side of life: what makes the heart pound, the adrenalin flow, the breath catch in the throat. And hoping always that the reader is having a frightfully good time, too."

Diane Hoh grew up in Warren, Pennsylvania. Since then, she has lived in New York, Colorado, and North Carolina, before settling in Austin, Texas. "Reading and writing take up most of my life," says Hoh, "along with family, music, and gardening." Her other horror novels include *Funhouse*, *The Accident*, *The Invitation*, *The Fever*, and *The Train*.

Return to Nightmare Hall
... *if you dare.*

*Wishes Granted, Fortunes Told.*

That was what the sign said on the mysterious booth at the back of Vinnie's pizzeria.

Alex was the first to notice the booth. Hidden in a dark alcove, it was tall and narrow. The bottom part was made of dark red metal, the top part glass, like a phone booth. At first Alex thought it was a phone booth, which was what she'd come looking for. Then she realized there was no phone inside. Curious, she walked over to get a better look.

And drew back in fear.

Inside the booth sat a figure. *The Wizard* it said on the glass.

He seemed made of stone, stiff and unmoving inside his red metal booth. His face was long and chiselled, his jaw firm, his painted mouth slightly open. His skin was pale ivory, his beard and mustache snowy-white. He wore a tall, pointed hat and a long, flowing gown to match.

But it was his eyes that Alex would always remember.

Made of glass, they were a deep, dark blue. Icy cold.

Terrifying.

It's just a mechanical fortune-teller, Alex told herself. A machine that claims it can make wishes come true.

Still, she couldn't shake the feeling that it was watching her . . .